ALL I NEED IS YOU

D. ROSE

MESSAGE FROM D. ROSE

Hi there,

Thank you for taking the time to read my second book! When I finished writing Autumn and Dean's story, I was a mix of emotions. I hope you enjoy their story as much as I enjoyed writing it. When you're done I kindly ask that you leave a review sharing your thoughts.

With love,
D.

ALL I NEED IS YOU

CONTENTS

utumn

DEAN and I were on our way from seeing a movie when we pulled up to his New Jersey townhouse. I was the first to notice the car parked across the street.

"Do you recognize that car?" I asked as he opened the door for me.

"No," was all he said as he grabbed my hand to usher me up the steps to his front door.

"Dean," a soft, raspy voice called out his name.

I turned around to a petite girl. Well, woman, but she looked no older than 25. She was light-skinned with long hair past her shoulders and I also noticed she had a

1

very round belly poking through the sweatshirt and leggings she wore. My eyes widened at the sight of her and I immediately looked to Dean who was just as shocked as I was. I searched his eyes for confirmation of whether or not he knew her. The exhale he released was all I needed to know. I let go of his hand, and I folded my arms over my chest. With my right eyebrow raised, I waited for him to try to explain himself.

"Can I have a minute to talk to her?" his eyes were pleading with me not to cause a scene. I stood there and said nothing as he concluded that I didn't mind if he talked to her. He walked over to her car shaking his head the entire time.

"Why are you here Liliana?" Frustration is evident in his voice.

Liliana.

I've seen her name in his phone a time or two. But I didn't feel it was my place to question who she is to him. We aren't officially together, so I thought I had no right to make it an issue.

"I've been calling you for weeks and no answer, so this was a last resort," she sniped at him. "I am pregnant, and the baby is yours." My mouth dropped at the same time as my arms.

"What?" Dean said as he ran his hand over his face.

"You heard me. I am pregnant. The night we met at your club is the night OUR baby was conceived." I stood speechless watching this encounter.

"How are you 100% sure that I am the father?" he leaned on her car while scratching the back of his ear.

"You're the only person I've been with since last year. You are the father, Dean. I am even willing to take a DNA test to prove it to you." She put her hands on her hips. "Look I just wanted you to know. I didn't make this baby by myself and I expect you to be there as much as possible." She pushed Dean off her car and opened the door. He grabbed her door before she closed it.

"Look, can we talk about this tomorrow? You out here at 2 am in my driveway like we are in the hood somewhere." He gritted his teeth. I heard enough. I pulled out my phone and requested a ride home.

"Well, if you would've answered my calls we wouldn't be doing this now would we? Move," she said, firmly. Dean stepped back as she closed her door in his face. Within minutes my ride was here. I walked past Dean and Liliana without making eye contact with either of them.

"Chubs," he called out after me.

Chubs, that's the name Dean gave me because of my fat cheeks. Any other time that would make me weak. But right now it was the last thing I wanted to hear. I ignored him calling after me as I closed the door and never looked back.

Two weeks later…

"Autumn open up!" Dean yelled as he banged on my

door. After two weeks of me avoiding him, I guess he'd reached his breaking point. I blocked his number this morning as I could no longer take him calling and texting all day and night.

"What Dean?" I spat after opening the door. He stood in front of me looking good, but I wasn't going to let that distract me, not today. After realizing I wasn't letting him in, he began apologizing again.

"Chubs, I am sorry about what happened with Liliana." I nodded for him to continue. "I had no idea she was pregnant. I dealt with her way before we ever met. You have to believe me, baby," he said, with sadness apparent in his eyes.

"Dean," I paused searching for the right words to say. "I believe you, but that doesn't change the fact that you indeed have a baby on the way. I'm not in a space to deal with all that right now."

"So, what are you saying?"

"Let's just be friends right now. I think that's best for the both of us," I folded my arms over my chest.

"You serious right now?" he flared his nostrils.

"Very."

As much as I wanted Dean to be the man I fall madly in love with, the man that helps me see that I am worthy of being loved unconditionally; he only reminds me of past hurt and abandonment I haven't fully healed from yet. We were moving way too fast, and this is a sign that we needed to slow down. I need to focus on me and fully recover from this open wound I have been trying to avoid. As I watched him walk back to his car defeated, I prayed I was making the right decision.

1

---

*D*ean

"DA-DA," Yara called out for me. My babygirl slapping her drool drenched hands on my face is how I started most of my mornings these days. I could always count on her to wake me up this way. I know she shouldn't be sleeping with me, especially since she had her room baby proofed and covered in pink and sparkles courtesy of the interior designer I hired. But I just like knowing she was within my reach. My king sized bed was perfect for the both of us. She slept with no problems, in fact, she was asleep by 8pm every night, getting her to stay asleep past 7am was the problem.

"Come on, babygirl. Give daddy 15 more minutes,"

7

I groaned, as I removed her wet hand from my face and covered my head with my pillow.

"No," she said, with a giggle. That was her favorite word. At least that's what she loved to tell me. No, mama, nana, and dada were all the words my one-year-old baby Yara, or Yaya as I like to call her, knew. She was the cutest baby I have ever seen. She got most of her physical traits from her mother. Her honey brown skin, big round eyes, and cute button nose were all compliments of Liliana. She had my dark brown coils and bad temper. We both are working on that. I picked babygirl up and headed towards the kitchen. There was no point in me trying to go to the bathroom first. Babygirl would follow me and burst in like always. I put her in the high chair before heading to my fridge to decide what I wanted to feed her. Liliana is a vegan, so she had me making Yaya fresh baby food with no milk, eggs, or meat. My baby loves bananas and spinach, so I mixed the two in a food processor before feeding her.

"Daddy needs to use the bathroom; I will be right back." I turned on her favorite show on her tablet before running to the bathroom. After brushing my teeth and washing my face, I looked at myself in the mirror. The barbershop was the first stop on my list after dropping Yara off with her mother because I barely recognize myself.

"Alright let's eat!" I kissed her forehead as I sat down in the chair in front of her high seat.

"Is it good, baby?" I asked, proud of my cooking skills. This year has been a never-ending learning process, but I think I finally have fatherhood down. Yara nodded her head yes as she wiped the excess food from her face.

After breakfast, I bathed and dressed her. The only thing I was still struggling with was how to do hair. Luckily Yara had a curly fro. So all I have to do is put some cream Liliana gave me on her hair, and we are good to go.

"Let's FaceTime mama," I said, grabbing my phone off the nightstand. Her face lit up with excitement. After two rings Lili picked up.

"Hi, mommy's baby," Lili yelled into the camera. Her shoulder length hair was in a big puff on the top of her head, and she had on her cat-eye framed glasses. I knew she was in her studying mode.

This past year was a learning experience for her as well. We had to figure out how to co-parent. There weren't any real feelings between us, so it made the process easier. During her pregnancy, we spent time getting to know one another better. She allowed me to be present at every doctor's appointment and for the birth of our daughter. The first month after Yara was born, I stayed with them at her house. Being able to form a genuine friendship with one another helped us with being first-time parents. She is a great mother to our daughter and has become a good friend of mine. We also have help from our mothers who are very happy and active grandmothers.

Lili graduated magna cum laude while being eight months pregnant with babygirl. She now works as a social worker's assistant and is going to school at night to get her master's degree. Although the circumstances weren't the best, I lucked up with having her as the mother of my child. She was younger than me, but she has herself together. We made a schedule that works well for the both of us. She has babygirl Thursday-Saturday, and I have her the other days unless something pops up. Lili had an event at school last night which is how I ended up keeping Yaya on a Friday evening.

I turned the camera on me, and Lili burst out laughing. "Wow you look rough," she said covering her mouth.

"Man, shut up. I'm getting my hair cut after I drop her off with you." I ran my hand over my hair.

"Good. My baby daddy can't be out here looking like that." She pointed in the camera.

"Yeah, yeah. How have you been tho'? How's school this semester?"

"I've been good. School is school." She rolled her eyes. "What time you have to be at Linx tonight?"

I looked up thinking about what time I wanted to get to the club.

"It all depends on how long the wait is at the

barbershop. I will probably go in around six. I won't be there long though because Grant's birthday dinner is tonight. What time are you leaving the library, nerd?"

She laughed and took her glasses off. "Right, I forgot Grant's dinner is tonight. I'm leaving in a few hours lets say two-ish. If you need to drop babygirl off early, my mom won't mind watching her."

"Nah, it's no problem. My partner in crime and I will be just fine. Ain't that right Yaya?" I said while planting kisses all over Yara's face while she chewed on the string of my basketball shorts.

"Alright, I will see you later let me say bye to my baby." I turned the camera back to Yaya so Lili could talk gibberish to her. Yara waved bye and so did I before ending the call.

I let Yara play in her room as I showered and dressed. I had a camera in her room that I monitored from my phone. She was playing with her baby piano and screaming some words that probably was to a song she made up. I laughed at her then continued to get dressed. I planned on taking her to the park to burn some of this energy off before taking her to Liliana's.

A call from Bre, the woman I'm currently dating, interrupted me checking on Yara for the hundredth time. I met her at the park while playing with babygirl. We've been dating for three months, she is a cool girl, but I don't know if I see myself in a relationship with her. She was just someone to occupy my time.

"Wassup?" I answered, and put the call on speakerphone so I could continue getting dressed.

"Are we still on for tonight?" Bre asked eagerly. Today is Grant's 35th birthday. Ivy is throwing him this lavish dinner party, and after she overheard Ivy and I talking about it, she asked if she could come.

"Yeah, I will pick you up after eight," I responded coolly.

"Ok, see you later, baby."

I shook my head as I disconnected the call. I told her early on I wasn't looking for a relationship or commitment. She was doing good at first, but now I can see her feelings are getting more vested. She calls to 'check-in' more, wants more attention, and she has been talking about G's birthday dinner for the past week. This would be the first time that Bre will be around my friends and family, but I still want her to understand that being my date for tonight isn't as big of a deal as she is making it out to be.

I went to babygirl's room and picked her up.

"Ready to go play baby?" I kissed her cheek as we headed out the door.

YARA WORE me out at the park, but I couldn't bail on G's dinner. This past year had been a very successful one for him. He got promoted, married, and is now a father. We opened a club in LA, and it was doing well considering it's only been open for a few months. We were able to get a few endorsements from celebrities, so that helped a lot too.

I looked over at Bre who was looking beautiful as always. Her dark skin looked amazing covered in the burgundy dress she is wearing; it was so tight it showed off her hourglass shape. Her long hair was straight with a middle part. My black suit and burgundy shirt matched her dress. We complimented each other perfectly. We walked into the private room Ivy booked at Grant's favorite restaurant. It looks like we are early, I didn't see any familiar faces as I looked around the room. The dimly lit room had a single long rectangular table directly in the center, covered by a white tablecloth. The centerpiece was a crystal vase with two dozen long stem red roses. Every place setting consisted of a clear glass plate with the menu on the center. I sat Bre down at the table before walking over to Ivy who was speaking with a waiter about the menu.

"Dean! It's so good to see you." Ivy gave me a tight hug. It has been a few weeks since I last saw them. They just welcomed baby Gabby who was born last month. Labor Day just passed, G and I usually have a big cookout, but I have been giving them space to be parents. The new addition to their family will take a lot of adjusting.

"It's good to see you too. You sure you just had a

baby?" I spun her around as she laughed at me. Ivy still looked the same except she filled out some from her pregnancy.

"Where is G?" I asked looking around the room, but everything went silent when Autumn walked in.

Autumn.

Damn. I had been trying my best not to think about that woman. Last year when she told me we could only be friends, she did everything to avoid me. Tonight is the first time I'd seen her in months. I accepted that this is how it would be. A man grabbing her waist from behind stopped my train of thought. *Did she bring a date too?* My brows wrinkled at the thought of her being with someone else. Her date looked like he was *artsy*. He had locs that were in a bun. *He isn't her type.*

"Dean," Ivy called my name.

"Yeah?" I cleared my throat and adjusted my tie.

"Grant is over there." She smiled while pointing in the opposite direction of where I was staring. She cocked her head to the side and smiled.

"Chill," was all I said as I walked towards G.

I walked over to Grant, but my eyes remained on Autumn. Everything about her is breathtaking. She had a natural glow about her. Her hair was in its naturally curly state down her back. She had on a black knee length dress that was off her shoulders. Her, buttery smooth skin glistened under the light, and her face is virtually make-up free. I knew because you could see the small moles on her face, they were so little they were often mistaken for freckles. Whatever her date was saying in her ear made her smile. Her cheeks rose as her teeth showed. Damn, I missed her. She must've felt me staring because she looked my way. The moment we made eye contact I watched her take in a deep breath. She instantly looked away and walked out of the room. I wanted to chase behind her and apologize again for hurting her.

"Happy birthday, G!" I dapped Grant into a hug.

"Thanks, bro. I'm getting old huh?"

"No doubt." We both laughed.

It was true we were getting old, but G is definitely in a great place in his life. He had a successful career, a supportive wife, and a beautiful babygirl. It was incredible to witness and seeing how great he is doing is indeed a motivation to let go of this player life. After we caught up on his life as a new father, we all sat down and prepared for the five-star meal Ivy curated for us. She had all of Grant's favorite foods from appetizers to dessert. Ivy even created a menu of drinks named after him. I couldn't help but smile as I watched Ivy and G interact with one another. The love they had was evident in everything they did together. Beside Ivy, Autumn is engaging in a conversation with her date. I stood to walk over to her, but Ivy thought I was about to make a toast, so she told everyone to quiet down. I picked up my almost empty glass of Henny and made up a speech on a whim.

"First, I want to say Ivy did the damn thing with this five-course meal. I am stuffed." I patted my stomach causing everyone to erupt in laughter. "Secondly, I want to wish my bro G a happy birthday. He is one of the most giving and hard working men I know. You deserve every good thing that comes your way. Especially that wife of yours." I winked at Ives, and she started clapping making everyone laugh again. "No, but seriously, let this be a lesson for all of us when you find the one do all you can to keep them." I looked at Autumn, and she looked away when we made eye contact. "To love and more life."

Everyone stood and repeated "love and more life," and toasted.

After dinner, everyone mingled on the balcony of the restaurant. I had a few glasses of Henny and feeling myself is an understatement. All night I had my eye on Autumn, and when her date stepped away, I took that as my chance to speak to her. She didn't know I was coming because her back was facing me. She was leaning on the rail staring at the view. I crept up behind her and whispered in her ear.

"Beautiful isn't it?" While being this close to her, the scent of brown sugar overwhelmed my nostrils as I licked my lips.

She tensed up before stepping to the side and turning

to face me. She looked me in my eyes with a blank face. I don't know whether she is surprised or pissed by me speaking to her. Either way, I decided I would continue the conversation.

"How have you been? It's been a while." I leaned on the railing waiting for her to respond. While I waited for her to respond, I took this time to get a good look at her. The form-fitting dress she wore accentuated her pear shape. I instinctively licked my lips while my eyes roamed her body freely. I ran the back of my hands down her arms, and I felt the chills that appeared on her skin. "Damn," I thought to myself as I took a step closer to her, and she stepped back.

She shook her head before replying, "I've been good, Dean." She folded her arms over her chest making me laugh while finishing the last of my drink.

"Why are you so cold towards me now?" Autumn is one of the sweetest and friendliest people I've ever met. So it confuses me how she can be so cold and distant towards me. She doesn't have a bad bone in her body.

I wanted to ask her why she stopped answering my calls and texts. Ask her how could I fix this, fix us. Before she could answer my question, her date came back. Dude put his arm around her waist trying to mark his territory. What he didn't know was Autumn is, and always will be, mine. I chuckled at him thinking he was intimidating me.

"I'm Dean, an *old* friend of Autumn's." She rolled her eyes at my sarcasm.

"I'm Rim, a *current* friend of hers." He extended his hand, and I shook it.

"Come on Rim. I am ready to go." Autumn grabbed his hand and practically dragged him out the door.

I went back inside to find Bre talking to Ivy. For some reason that annoyed me. I didn't need her telling Ivy anything that could get back to Autumn or exaggerate what was going on between us. I could tell by the look on Ivy's face; she felt relieved that I was coming to end their pointless conversation.

"Bre, you ready to go?" I asked trying to mask my annoyance with her.

"Not yet, I'm getting to know Ivy. She is telling me about her babygirl, Gabby. I hope to meet her soon." Ivy looked at me and squinted her eyes.

"After I say bye to G, we are leaving," I said with finality. I walked away with Ivy close behind me.

"I didn't know you had a girlfriend?" Ivy said with a light chuckle.

"I don't." My face went from relaxed to a scowl. That girl was over there telling Ivy anything.

"That's not what she said. She has met Yara and everything. Why haven't you mentioned her to us?" She grabbed my arm making me stop in my tracks. Ivy and I have formed a close bond since she was now the wife of my cousin. She was practically like a little sister.

However, I was still careful about what I shared with her because she knows I still have feelings for Autumn and I know she tells her things about me.

I grabbed Ivy by the shoulders. "Listen, she is not my girlfriend. We date and have sex. That is it. When we first met, I was at the park with babygirl that's the only time she has been around her. I wouldn't just bring anyone around my baby. You know me better than that."

"What's going on here?" Grant asked as walked over to us. Ivy and I filled him in on what happened, and he laughed. "Well, what are you going to do?" Grant asked before sipping his drink.

"I don't know." I ran my hand over my face in frustration.

"Well, whatever you do make sure you think before you act. We all know how that temper of yours is." I nodded taking in everything G said. He has always been my voice of reason since we were young boys. We shared our byes before I grabbed Bre to leave.

The car ride to Bre's house was quiet, if it wasn't for the noise from the radio it would've been complete silence. I was trying to think of a way to calmly express my disapproval of her telling Ivy those lies. Trying to make us seem more than what we are. When we passed the exit I usually take to get to my house, she turned to me and pressed her lips together to keep from saying anything and went back to being on her phone.

I pulled into her driveway and parked the car. When

I didn't unbuckle my seatbelt, she knew I wasn't ending my night with her. She turned in her seat towards me.

"Wassup Dean? You've been acting weird all night. First, you ignore me at dinner. Then, I spot you talking to that girl you were staring at all night. What, are you going to see her after you leave here?" Bre had worked my last nerve tonight.

"I think we need to chill for a bit. You are catching feelings, and I told you from the jump that's not what I'm on." Bre huffed and folded her arms over her chest. I let her pout for about 30 seconds before unlocking the door.

"I'll hit you up later on." I looked straight ahead as she got out of my car with an attitude. She cursed me under my breath. That was fine. As long as she didn't say anything slick to me, we were good. I pulled out of her driveway and turned the music up and cruised the rest of the way home.

$\mathcal{A}$utumn

I CAN'T BELIEVE Dean had the nerve to talk to me like everything is all good. After abruptly leaving Grant's birthday dinner, I had Rim bring me home. I reached my boiling point. Everything Dean said or does gets under my skin. Unfortunately, the break I took from being around him didn't help like I thought it would. I needed to get to my canvas as soon as possible since the distraction of creating art is the only way I would sleep peacefully tonight. Since I was a child, this has been my way of expressing my feelings. My idea of keeping a diary was through my artwork. My pencil connecting with my canvas erased all the thoughts running through my head. If I didn't have my pencil or a brush in my hand, I honestly didn't feel alive. I don't know what I would do if I couldn't create. Over the years painting had become more than a hobby or talent. It was my therapy. My reason to get out of bed every day. The reason I won't take a job that doesn't allow me to use my gift to help others.

Art is my life.

The painting I am doing for my ray of sunshine, my Godchild Gabby is the perfect distraction. This piece is very special to me because Gabby is my heart in human form. The day she was born, and I looked into those hazel eyes and it was love at first sight. For the past month, I have been going to see her daily. She was the perfect way to end each day. When Ivy first told me about her pregnancy, I was caught off guard, hurt, and happy all at the same time. It bothered me because of my own selfish reasons. Mainly due to me still grieving over the loss of my baby. Ivy is the sister I've always wanted, so I put my feelings aside to be there for her. I knew she would need me like I needed her. Every day, I prayed she would have a healthy, non-complicated pregnancy because I would never wish what I went through on anyone. Ivy also had a great husband by her side through it all. I applaud Grant for being patient with my stubborn sister. 'Cause Lord knows she doesn't listen to anyone but herself.

I didn't want my thoughts to completely consume

me, so I focused on the outline that I've just finished and started lining my bottles of paint up in the order that I wanted them on my palette. The painting was going to be a portrait of Ivy holding Gabby. I snuck and took the picture one day when I was visiting. The moment I saw it I knew that's the gift I wanted to give her. For this special piece, I used the brush set Ives had gotten me as a gift. For months I talked about these brushes, and after I accepted the role of Godmother, she gave them to me as a thank you.

For two hours I painted as Jill Scott's first album played in the background. My legs were beginning to feel sore letting me know I had been standing too long. So I took a seat on the floor of my art studio and drank a glass of wine I poured. I looked at my distressed overalls taking notice of the paint I had inadvertently gotten all over myself. Like my many other pairs of overalls, these would now only be used for painting and art projects. I took a quick picture of my piece and sent it to Grant. Usually, I don't show my work until it's completed, but for Grant, I made an exception, he was just as excited about it as I was. He sent a reply saying it was dope and that I was dope too. I laughed while putting my phone away.

Since sleep still isn't in my near future, I prepared lesson plans for the upcoming school week. Although I have bigger dreams, I genuinely love teaching art. Some of my students were taking the class to graduate, and some have the love for art, the same fire I had when I was a teen. The immense amount of joy I feel when watching and pushing my students to create in any way they deem healthy is what keeps me teaching. I have so many folders and boxes full of my students artwork at my house that when I finally get my gallery, I plan on displaying all of their work. Last year, I told myself I was going to quit teaching and be an artist full time, but I am my own worst enemy. Researching all the costs that come along with owning an art gallery, discouraged me from pursuing my dream. So, for now, I am still teaching and selling art on the side until I can gain the courage to start my business.

However, I am still hosting showcases to keep my name relevant in the art community. I will be displaying a series I worked on in an upcoming art showcase. My nerves were starting to get the best of me because these pieces were darker than what I am used to. However, when I painted these pieces last summer, I was in a dark space in my life. Like I said before, my artwork is my diary. My longtime friend Rim convinced me to submit these pieces because they are different from my past series. He always pushed me to step outside my comfort zone, so I listened.

Rim.

We met in college in an art class and been cool ever since. There has always been an attraction between us. I mean what is there not to be attracted to? His caramel colored skin, long brown locs, and big pink lips were enough to have women lusting over him. However, it was never the right time. Throughout college, I was in a long-term relationship, and he was engaged to his high school sweetheart until our senior year. Now that we were both single and in a great place in our lives we decided now was a better time than ever. We recently had a conversation and decided maybe we could explore this attraction and see where it leads us. It's only been about a month, but so far everything has been good. I thought the run-in he had with Dean would cause some questions to arise, but he was cool about it. In fact, he didn't bring it up, and I was glad because I didn't have the energy to explain our past.

After I found out Dean had a baby on the way I cut him off. I wasn't interested in baby mama drama or whatever other baggage came along with it. When I said I wanted to be friends, Dean took that very seriously. I did, I mean I do wish to be his friend, but him having a baby at the same time we were trying to get to know one another bothered me. It didn't help that he called and texted nonstop. Honestly, I wasn't able to put the fast-growing feelings I had for him aside to be just friends. After two months of me ignoring him, he got the hint and stop reaching out. Ivy gave me unwanted updates on his life every now and then. She too was going hard for me to give Dean another chance. Sometimes I feel like I owe Dean some type of explanation for why I had to distance myself from him. However, I wasn't ready to face the demons I was avoiding and being with Dean would make me confront that head-on. Ivy feels the need to let me know he still checks on me. It felt good to know even though I pushed him away I was still on his mind. For the first time in months, I was letting Dean consume my thoughts. Unfortunately, he had that effect on me.

You are not going down that road again. I thought to myself.

Still not feeling the urge to go to sleep, I ran my bath water and lit some aromatherapy candles. While soaking in the tub, my thoughts about my upcoming busy week and art show filled my head. Although I was a tad bit anxious, the warmth of the water and the scent of chamomile invading my nostrils put me into a relaxed state.

I WIPED the sweat from my forehead as I finished the last mile of my morning run. The past two April's I've participated in a 5k for heart disease in memory of my mother. Training for those marathons gave me a new way to relieve stress and tone up. My running buddy was still recuperating from childbirth, so my morning runs have been done solo. Some days I miss hearing Ivy complain about how I'm running too fast or trying to cut our route short. The list of excuses she would come up with caused a quiet chuckle to escape my lips. As much as she claimed to hate running I could always count on her to be at my house at 5:30 am sharp.

Once I made it back home, I showered and dressed for the day. Being an art teacher had its perks as far as dress code was concerned, being able to dress comfortably was the most important one. Today I was channeling my inner Nola Darling by wearing a white head-wrap and oversized button up and a pair of boyfriend jeans. These jeans had paint stains on them which was perfect because today my students will be painting color wheels. It is still the beginning of the school year, so the material I had to cover was pretty dull in my opinion. However, I found ways to make the lessons plan interactive because I am not going to be that teacher to stand and read from a book.

After getting dressed I checked my phone, and as always Rim sent me a sweet text to get my day started on the right foot. Unlike me, he quit his job and followed his dream of being an artist full time. Rim often traveled with well-known poets to paint while they performed, it was a dope concept and it didn't hurt that he enjoys traveling from city to city meeting new people. When he's home, Rim is teaching art classes at the local community center. I sent him back a cute text wishing him a great day. The school I worked at was about 4 blocks from my place. The summer weather was still in effect well into September, so I decided to walk this morning. I knew Ivy would be up either working or feeding Gabby, so I called them to talk.

"Good morning," I sang into my headphone mic.

Ivy yawned in response, "Good morning, girl." She sounds like she didn't get any sleep last night.

"Long night?" I asked.

"Yes very. Gabby had a hard time staying asleep last night. Grant and I alternated waking up every two hours. I've been sitting in this rocking chair since 5am."

"Damn. I will be over as soon as the school day ends. You want me to bring by some food too?"

"Yes, please. You are the best." I heard the smile in her voice.

"I know," I responded cockily. "I just got to work, see you later." After disconnecting the call, I put my bags down on my desk and opened the blinds to allow sunlight in, highlighting the fact that the walls of my classroom are still bare. I can't wait until my students start to do more hands-on work so I can cover the paint chipped walls. After writing this weeks mantra on the whiteboard, I stepped back and read it aloud. "*I am one of a kind, and my gifts cannot be duplicated.*" I placed the purple marker back in my pen holder. Now I am ready to start my day.

GOING to Ivy's house during rush hour was a bad idea. It slipped my mind that she no longer lives in the city. When she and Grant got married, they moved to the suburbs, I guess that's what happens when you get married and start a family. You move out of the busy city to the quiet and boring suburbs. After sitting in traffic for what felt like forever, I pulled into their middle-class neighborhood. All of the houses looked like mini-mansions, this is definitely a family-centered development. After I punched in the code to their gate, I drove up their long driveway, parked my car and grabbed the bags of Chinese food I picked up for us before heading to the door. Minutes after ringing the doorbell, I was greeted by a still tired Ivy and a sleeping Gabby. Ivy led us to the living room; I took a seat on their sectional sofa while she placed Gabby in her bassinet.

"I am so glad you are here." She leaned down and hugged me. "Let me go grab us some plates and forks." She walked to the kitchen. When she returned she plated our food for us. "How was your day?" Ives asked before sticking a fork full of fried rice in her mouth.

"It was great. I can't complain." I shrugged. "Where is Grant?" I asked after realizing I hadn't seen or heard him.

"He had a few meetings today. I told him if I have to cut back on work he does too. So today will be his last day working for a few weeks. I need him here with

Gabby and me. I have been walking around like a zombie all day. My mom suggested I start giving her baths in lavender oil to help her wind down because I can't keep having nights like last night." Gabby squirmed in her bouncer making us pause our conversation and watch for her next move. Ivy checked the time on her phone.

"It's time for her to eat again."

She was about to get up when I stopped her. "No, you eat. I will make Gabby's bottle and feed her." Ivy exhaled as she leaned back on the sofa.

"Thank you so much. I need a minute to just breathe."

"No worries. After you eat, go take a hot bath. I will watch Gabby for you."

Ivy's eyes watered. "You are the best sister anyone could ask for," I knew it was her hormones making her emotional.

"You know I would do anything for you." After I fed Gabby, I gave her a bath and sang her the lullabies my mom used to sing to me, while rocking her to sleep. I must admit having a Godchild has helped me cope with the loss of my baby boy. I thought I would be resistant to being around her but to my surprise, I am the complete opposite. Last summer, Ivy referred me to her therapist after I shared my reservations about being a Godmother. Going to see Dr. Lewis helped me realize I wasn't the cause of my miscarriage and that there was nothing wrong with my body. Those were the lies that regularly played in my mind. I also got some closure from being abandoned by my ex while I was grieving. After laying Gabby in her crib covering her with the blanket Grant's mom made, I went to check on Ivy she had fallen asleep while in the tub. Not wanting to wake her, I went back to the living room and sketched on my pad. About 30 minutes later Ivy came downstairs looking refreshed.

"How was your nap?" I closed my pad and put it away.

"It was great. Thanks again for coming over and helping out."

"Stop," I said while waving my hand. "I have to go. I will see you this weekend at my art show."

"Of course, we wouldn't miss it for the world." Ivy grinned. We shared a tight hug then I headed home.

After I arrived home, I undressed into a pair of yoga shorts and a baby tee. I sat in the middle of the floor in my art studio with my legs folded. My art showcase is this weekend, I'm still trying to shake my nerves. This is the first time I would be showing a large number of people work I did at a very vulnerable point in my life. The question about how I came up with the theme for this series haunts me the most. Although I have gone through the proper channels to heal that wound, I am not fully open to talking about it just yet. Sitting with my legs crossed, I admired the paintings that lined the walls, from the silhouette of a pregnant woman to the young boy crying all these paintings meant so much to me. My train of thought was disrupted by my phone ringing. The name that appeared on the screen made my stomach turn. I knew once I came face to face with Dean again this would happen. After ignoring the first two calls, I answered the third time, a part of me was anxious to hear what he has to say after all this time of no communication.

"Yes, Dean?" I rolled my eyes. My heart was pounding so hard against my chest anxiously awaiting to hear his voice. The agitation in my voice didn't match the sense of nervousness overcoming me.

"Damn, is this how it is now?" he chuckled nervously. I walked over to the window and gazed at the moon. He let out a long breath before continuing, "You really don't fuck with me anymore, huh?"

"I think you know the answer to that, Dean," I said, becoming less anxious and more agitated by the minute.

"Listen, I didn't call you to argue or anything like that. It was good seeing you the other day. And again I'm sorry, Autumn. I don't know what else to say or do," Dean said with a hint of sadness in his tone. I leaned against the wall and looked down, with my right leg crossed over the right, I exhaled.

"I don't know either," I murmured.

"Let's go to dinner and talk about this," he said calmly. His calmness was pissing me off. The nerve of him to think that he could call me up and invite me to dinner! Meanwhile, I'm hating myself for losing control of my emotions just from hearing Dean's voice.

"There's nothing to talk about," I cut him off. "I think it's best that we..."

"Just be friends? Yeah, you said that already," he hissed.

"No, I think it's best we keep doing what we've been doing, not talking. Plus, I saw your date. You have a girlfriend or whatever she is. Your hands seem full."

He chuckled, "Ok, Autumn. I will talk to you later." Dean hung up before I could have the last word. I slammed my phone down on the table next to me. *Why is it that he can get me upset like this?* I let out a hard breath as my shoulders slumped. This is why I have been avoiding him all this time. My feelings for him are still lingering in the background no matter how hard I try to avoid them.

3

*D*ean

"THERE IS MY BEAUTIFUL GRANDBABY," my mother reached to take Yaya from my arms. I had to bring her over so my mom could watch her while I worked tonight. We had two players from the Nets coming to host, so I had to make sure everything was in order.

"Damn, your only son can't get no love?" I asked while putting Yaya's bags down on the kitchen counter.

"Boy hush," she hugged me and kissed my cheek. After my mother put Yaya down, she walked into the living room to her toy box.

"Thanks for watching her last minute. I forgot Lili

was going out of town this weekend." I took a seat at the dining room table.

"You know watching my grandbaby is never an inconvenience." She waved her hand at me. I went into the fridge to grab the glass pitcher filled with her infamous lemonade. After pouring us both glasses, I took a seat next to her. There was a lingering silence between us which only meant one thing, my mother was about to bring up something she knew would piss me off.

Before breaking the silence, my mother took a long sip. "Did you call your father like I asked?" she sat the cup down on the table. Here we go with this again. My parents divorced five years ago because my father was cheating on my mom with his young ass secretary. The hurt he caused my mother made me resent him to no end. How could you step out on a woman who had been holding you down for almost 30 years? "You need to forgive your father. You've gone long enough without speaking to him. He has been trying to mend you alls relationship for years. I forgave him a long time ago and you should too."

My mother has always been 'the peacemaker,' nothing makes my mother happier than everyone being happy and getting along. However, she never forced me to mend my estranged relationship with my father until Yaya. She is his first and only grandchild. I don't know if I want him to be in her life. Shit, I don't know if I want him to be in mine ever again.

I blew out a breath. "Come on, Ma, you know I didn't call him." I ran my hand over my face. "Look I have to go to Linx. I will come back tomorrow to pick up babygirl."

She grabbed my arm. "We aren't done with the conversation, Silas." Her calling me by my middle name made me cringe. She knows I despise that name. That was her way of warning me that her patience is wearing thin.

"For real, I'm not in the mood to talk about this right now. I can't go to work with this situation on my mind. We can talk about this another time, promise." With that, I kissed both of my ladies bye before leaving. I had to get out of there before she started lecturing me. It's been five years and all of a sudden she wants me to reconnect with him. The entire car ride to the club I had flashbacks of the divorce process, thoughts of the first time my mother confronted my father about his indiscretions invaded my mind.

I came over for our weekly dinner. When I entered their house, I felt the tension. My mother was in the kitchen cooking on the verge of tears while my father watched a football game. "Ma, what's wrong?" I grabbed her shoulder.

"Nothing, baby." She quickly wiped away a tear. Her answer didn't satisfy me, so I went to ask my father

why my mother was crying. When I walked into the living room, my father was sitting in his black leather reclining chair with his feet kicked up. His expression held no emotion. He only looked like this when he was in deep thought.

"Pops, what's wrong with Ma? She is in there on the verge of tears," I said while pointing towards the kitchen.

He shrugged and continued to watch the game. The vibe in this house was so off, but I couldn't force them to tell me what was wrong. I took a seat on the couch and watched the game until dinner was ready. We ate dinner in complete silence, I looked back and forth between my parents as they ate. My mother never took her eyes off her plate. Her eyes still held tears as she fought them back. I looked at my father as he ate with a blank expression. After taking a sip of my lemonade, I looked at my mother.

"Ma, what is going on?" I grabbed her chin making her look up.

She looked across the table at my father with tears falling from her eyes. "Ask your father about Brooke."

"Brooke? His secretary?" I asked while turning to my father.

"Yes," my mother yelled out. She slammed her fists down on the table. "Ask him about the business trips he's been taking her on, the hotel rooms he's booked with her, and the emails about them discussing their *sexual escapades throughout his office." My mother now screaming to the top of her lungs. "Thirty years I have devoted to you. And you throw it away for someone half your age!" She stormed out of the dining room leaving only my father and me. While my mother exposed the secret life my father was living, I went completely numb. After she left the room I started to feel again, my heart was beating violently against my chest.*

"Yo, tell me it's not true," I gritted. "Tell me you haven't been doing mom like this?" I stood from my seat. My father sat there staring at his plate. When he didn't respond, I knew everything my mother said was true.

Shortly after that dinner, my mom moved into my two-bedroom apartment with me because she wanted to get away from my father. I was a 28-year-old bachelor who had to move his mother in because his father couldn't keep his dick in his pants. My grip on the steering wheel tightened thinking about all the drama he caused. If I never spoke to that man again, I would be just fine.

I SCANNED the crowd of Linx and was pleased, owning successful clubs has always been my dream. In college, I started out as a party promoter, then a host, and now I own three clubs. While in school I was so into the club scene that I changed my major from public policy to business administration. My parents were pissed which was expected, they didn't think I would be serious about running a business. They thought I was too young for the nightlife industry. However, I was able to prove them wrong. A significant part of the reason I was able to open my first lounge, Redstone, so young was because my mother had a trust fund set up for me at birth. I wasn't able to access the money until I was 25. Looking back on it I am glad she chose that age. Anything younger I would've blown it trying to impress girls. I used half to open Redstone and after seeing how good it was doing, I opened Linx two years later. My dream is to own a club in every major city and vacation spot in the U.S. Redstone and Linx hold New York City down, while YaYa's Place is located in the center of the Hollywood's nightlife. The overwhelming success of YaYa's Place has made that dream seem more feasible than in the past. RedStone is more of a hip-hop club, rappers come there to perform and host. Where Linx is more grown and sexy, the crowd is late 20's on most weekends. During the week, we hold happy hour socials and I am working to make food a part of the happy hour socials aside from the chips and salsa we offer. After much convincing from my team, we decided to provide hostings at Linx. So far it hasn't taken away business from RedStone like I feared. In fact, both were doing great.

"Send another bottle of champagne to table 403," I told Shay, one of the bottle girls.

"You got it, boss." She went behind the bar and grabbed a bottle and sparklers before going towards the section I had the Nets players sitting. I made sure to have their table front and center so they could be the main attraction. That's what these young ballers wanted anyway, to be the center of attention.

After gazing at the dance floor taking in the scene, my eyes landed on the last person I expected to see, Bre. She was in VIP with two of her friends dancing. A part of me knew she came here to see me. That's the only time she came to my clubs. She wasn't a city type of girl. She spent a lot of her time across the bridge. I took a deep breath before walking over to her table. As I stood in front of their couch, I put my hands in my pockets. While she was dancing, I took the time to appreciate her beauty. Bre had on this short dress that barely covered anything, and her hair was in a ponytail. She looked good as hell, but that doesn't negate that we were on pause for right now.

I grabbed her waist while whispering in her ear, "Follow me."

She turned around smiling from ear to ear. Bre grabbed my hand as I led her to my office so we could talk. I closed the door, and she took a seat in the chair behind my desk. This girl is really something else.

"You want my attention. Now you have it." I stood

at the front of my desk with my arms folded. She bit her bottom lip as she slowly looked me up and down. I watched as she ran her tongue over her top lip. Clearly, she had a lot to drink tonight.

"You haven't called me in a week," she said, crossing her legs on my desk. I licked my lips at the sight of her chocolate thighs exposed on the mahogany wood. Bre knew what she was doing. Not being gullible to the bait in front of me, I took a seat in one of the available chairs.

"I told you we needed space. Then, you stormed out of my car slamming my door. Remember that?" I tapped my hand on the armrest of my chair. "Why would I call you after that little tantrum?" She stood up and walked over to me. After she sat down in my lap, she wrapped her arms around my neck.

"Yes, I remember. I'm sorry for that tantrum, but I miss you." Bre started kissing my neck. It was clear what she missed all right. She came in here with this small ass dress tipsy. I wasn't going to fall for the game she was trying to play. The way she acted at G's dinner turned me off from her for good. I moved her out of my lap and stood.

"Bre you're a very beautiful..." I looked her body over before continuing, "...woman, but this isn't going to work." I put my hands in my pockets and looked down.

"What do you mean it's not going to work?" she put her hand on her hip, "It's been working all this time.

There's someone else isn't it?" Bre rolled her neck with her finger in my face. Feeling the anger in her tone, I took a step back.

"We were never serious Bre, so stop. I told you this was supposed to be something chill. That's obviously not what you want. Telling my fam we were more than we are wasn't cool, and it didn't get you any points with Ivy. Bragging about being around my daughter wasn't ok either. I don't play when it comes to Yara." I shrugged before walking to my office door and opening it, "You can go back to enjoying your night with your girls." Bre opened her mouth to speak. I raised my eyebrow waiting for her to say some bullshit, but instead, she brushed past me and stormed out of my office. By the time I made it back to the VIP section, she was rushing her friends out of the front door. I shook my head. *That came and went fast.*

Grant's advice on just focusing on my business and Yara replayed in my head. "*Being the best father you can be and running these clubs should be your top priority. You still have a lot of growing to do. Focus on you, man.*" He said that to me the day Yara was born. My dating life slowed down once I became a father, he was right. I still have a lot of growing to do, and I'm really in no space to be entertaining anyone. Especially since I can't get...I shook thoughts of the name I've been trying to forget from my mind. She made it clear she wanted nothing to do with me, yet I was still having a hard time believing that. Her reaction when she saw me at Grant's birthday dinner showed me all I needed to know. But I was still unsure about how I could get us back on good terms.

"Boss," Shay called pulling me out of my thoughts. "We need you at the bar."

"Coming."

MY MOTHER ASKED to keep babygirl for the remainder of the weekend which I had no problem with. Now that I have some free time I can get my haircut. G and I haven't had a chance to chop it up since his party, so he met me at the shop. After going a month without a cut, it was time to get back on my weekly appointments.

"Wassup, G?" I dapped him as he was in the chair getting his cut. I sat in the chair next to him. My barber put the cape around my neck before spinning me around to the mirror.

"Nothing much, man. Ives got me going to Autumn's art showcase tonight." He looked at me out the corner of his eye.

I cleared my throat at the mention of her name. Since Grant's birthday dinner I had been trying to keep her off my mind. After our conversation last week I got the feeling she was done with me for good. Secretly, I hoped us seeing each other would change our current status to at least being on speaking terms again. Sadly, I was proven wrong.

"You should come thru. Your girl has been working really hard preparing for it. Check out this piece she is doing for Gabs." He pulled out his phone. The portrait of Ivy holding Gabby was beautiful, and she wasn't even finished. Autumn is truly gifted, I've never seen anyone who is as sick with the brush as she is. That's one thing I miss about her, watching her in her element. I could sit and watch her paint for hours. Whenever she had a brush in her hand, there was a twinkle in her eye that couldn't be ignored. Painting really was her peace, her passion. Knowing that I will never be able to watch her in her element had my smile dropping. Feelings that I have been trying to tuck away were starting to arise, shit. I handed Grant his phone back.

"I don't think that's a good idea, man. Especially after the way she stormed out of your dinner when I tried to talk to her." I shook my head while thinking about how she dragged homeboy up out of there.

"What happened with that?" he inquired. I told him about our short conversation. "I don't think they're serious. At least that's what Ives said. They go back to their college days," he said unenthused, "But for real, come thru. Show her you still support her."

"I talked to her last week after the party. If she wanted me there, she would've invited me then."

"True, but maybe it slipped her mind," he shrugged.

"Nah, the conversation was anything but pleasant. Chubs answered the phone clearly in defense mode. So like I said, I don't think me coming tonight is best. All I know is I miss that woman, and she doesn't seem to feel the same." Saying I missed her out loud felt weird, but I know I can be open with G, and not have it held against me.

"Autumn is sweet, she can't keep up this tough girl front with you too much longer." We both laughed. That was very true she wasn't the type to stay mad or hold a grudge. Which is why I am so perplexed at how she has stayed mad at me for this long.

"Yeah, that's true. Send me the details and I will come." I sat back thinking about how Autumn would feel about me coming to her art show. Truthfully, I wanted to see her again, but I couldn't shake the feeling that she was avoiding seeing me or something. Although I was hurt when she first told me we could be nothing more than friends, I still did whatever I had to do to remain in her life while showing her I was apologetic for the way she found out about Yaya. Last summer, I fervently reached out to her to hang out like friends do. She ignored every single call and text I sent her for two months straight. I took her ignoring me as she didn't want shit to do with me. I chalked it up and moved on. Well, I tried...I mean I'm trying to move on.

Standing outside Espresso, I tried to shake the nervousness overcoming me. I bought Autumn a bouquet of lilies and a card, inside was a gift card so she could buy more art supplies. Although I'm sure, she doesn't need it. She had every color paint you could think of tubs full of it. After taking a deep breath, I went inside. The venue was bigger than I thought. There are so many people here I was having a hard time finding Autumn. Usually, I could spot her by her hair, but she changes styles so much. I continued to walk around while taking in the paintings she had posted throughout. Everything was beautiful, there was a painting of a young child crying. The child was black, and the tears were yellow. It was almost like a silhouette. Most of the pieces were dark, she only used black, blues, and purples. My favorite one was her ode to the movie, *Moonlight*. Autumn painted the movie poster with the three actors that played the main character. After about 10 minutes of walking around, I sat down at a table near the front door. It was almost Yaya's bedtime, so I called my mother to wish her a good night.

"Why are you calling me so late?" she huffed into the phone.

"Ma, it's only 7 pm," I laughed while leaning against the brick wall of the coffee shop. "Where is my baby?"

"I already put her down for the night. I gave her a warm bath, and she was out in no time," she bragged.

"You have to tell me your secret bath time routine 'cause I swear that never works for me."

"Nope, if I tell you I have to kill you," she laughed.

"What are you doing? Heading to the club soon?" I turned to look inside the window I saw Autumn walking through the room smiling and shaking hands of her guests. Autumn Richardson is everything, the way she floated through the crowd with her beautiful smile on full display made a smile appear on my face. Her high cheekbones made it look like her eyes were closed. My mouth started to water at the sight of the dress that is hugging her figure. So captivated by her, I almost forgot I was on the phone with my mother.

"I'm at an art show. Autumn's art show." I smiled. My teeth dug into my bottom lip as my eyes continued to follow her as she moved through the room.

"Autumn! I miss that girl. How is she? What ever happened with Y'all? I just knew she was going to be my daughter-in-law," she joked. That was my cue to end the call. I never told my mother the reason why we 'broke up.' Although, I'm sure she knows Liliana's pregnancy played a part in it.

"Ma, I have to go back inside. I will pick Yaya up tomorrow afternoon." I disconnected the call eager to get back to see her before she disappeared again.

4

*A*utumn

WHILE TALKING to a group of potential buyers about a piece, I became distracted. My heart dropped to my stomach. My eyes have to be deceiving me. There was no way Dean is at my art show. How did he even know about it? I looked over at Grant and Ivy who were too busy with one another to notice my evil glare. I told Ives a long time ago to stop trying to reconnect us. For the past year, I have been trying to purge this man from my heart. I did all I could to rid him from my mind and soul. And I still haven't entirely gotten over him. This was my second time seeing him this month, and it was too soon. The past year I managed to limit my interactions with him. If Grant and Ivy had an event, and I knew he would be there, I would either leave early or not show up at all. So seeing Dean at my art showcase made me feel...shit, I don't even know.

He finally found me after looking around the room for a few seconds. When we locked eyes, he let out a sigh of relief with a small smile as he made his way over to me. I ran my hands down my dress while taking in deep breaths. After excusing myself from the group, I slowly met Dean halfway. This man had butterflies moving through my stomach and my heart beating rapidly. I internally shook my head as I thought about the hold he still managed to have over me, over my heart. As we walked towards one another, I found myself taking the time to appreciate the man before me. Dean wore a white long sleeved button down shirt and a pair of dark wash jeans. Thanks to years of running track in high school and college, his athletic stature was still prominent. He wasn't overly muscular, but the definition showed in his arms and thighs. My favorite feature is his height, at 6'3 he towered perfectly over my 5'6 frame. His freshly cut hair and trimmed beard caused me to salivate with desire. His almond-shaped eyes showed the excitement his face was trying to mask.

"Can we talk outside for a minute?" he asked, gazing into my eyes intensely.

I wanted to say no but, "Sure" fell from my lips before I knew it. I led Dean through the back of the coffee shop and strategically placed a rock in the door to keep us from being locked out. For a moment we stood in the alley in silence. The silence wasn't awkward, it allowed both of us to find the right words to say to one another, my eyes wandered everywhere to avoid making eye contact with him.

"Congratulations on your art show Chu-" he cleared his throat. "I mean Autumn." Dean's smooth deep voice was better than my favorite song playing on repeat. A part of me wanted to hear him say the nickname he'd given me while dating. But I know that would have brought back memories... memories that I have been trying to erase. He handed me a bouquet of lilies, and a card then moved closer to hug me. Skeptically, I accepted his hug and melted right into him. I felt so comfortable in his arms I forgot where I was. Feelings that didn't need to arise made me break our embrace. His left hand grazed my arm, and I shivered.

"Thank you. You didn't have to do all this," I said, earnestly. I took another step back and leaned against the brick wall, being this close to him had me feeling some type of way.

"Of course I did. I have to support you because that's what *friends* do right?" he retorted with a sly smile. The emphasis he put on '*friends*' made me smile, but the smile quickly faded when I realized the reality of our situation.

We were anything but *friends*.

Friends talked frequently.

Friends hung out occasionally.

Friends got invites to events held for and by one another.

By no means were we *friends*. The reality of our situation caused a wave of sadness to come over me.

I smelled the lilies before responding, "Right," while forcing a smile. We had to end this conversation before I said or did something I would soon regret. I'm usually one to use logic over emotion, but when it comes to what the heart truly wants all logic goes out the window.

"I'm proud of you. Everything looks amazing, and I can tell you spent a lot of time working on this series," his eyes brightened before a smile tugged at the corner of his mouth.

My heart fluttered wildly at the sight of his smile.

"Thank you, I appreciate that," I looked down to hide the fact that I was starting to blush. *Get it together Autumn,* I yelled internally. "I have to get back to my guests if you see anything you want to let me know. I will give you a good deal." I winked and opened the door to head back inside. He grabbed my hand to stop me.

"I already know what I want." The seriousness in his tone had me stopping in my tracks. I wanted to turn around and say my rebuttal. Instead, I pulled my hand out of his and walked away. There was no way we were about to have this conversation again face to face. Over the phone, I can keep it together. But seeing the sadness in his eyes and feeling the warmth of his body near mine would have me falling back into his arms without a second thought.

For the rest of the night, Dean kept his distance, but I still caught him stealing glances from time to time. When Rim came back from catching up with an old coworker, he came up behind me and hugged me. Jealousy was all over Dean's face, his jaw clenched tightly, and his nostrils flared. Their first encounter was awkward and the tension between them was so thick. I would do anything to make sure that didn't happen again. Grabbing Rim's hand, I led him to the front of the coffee shop because there was no telling what Dean would do next.

"I'm so proud of you, babe." Rim pushed a loose curl from my face to behind my ear before he cupped my cheek. He leaned down to kiss me and reluctantly I accepted. Unlike kisses in the past, this one didn't hold the passion and warmth. I was outside kissing someone that I knew would make a great boyfriend and life partner, but the man I really wanted to be with was inside.

At one point in time, I was sure Dean was my soulmate, the instant magnetic attraction I felt for him caused me to think he was the one. However, could Dean really be my soulmate? The turn of events that caused our separation made me reconsider. Could that connection we shared be duplicated with someone else? Could I feel the same way about Rim as I once did Dean? Rim and I have so much in common. Rim is safe, I knew what to expect from him, and I felt comfortable giving him my heart. But with Dean back on my mind again it was hard to focus on what I was trying to build with Rim. After our moment we went back inside so I could continue to tend to my guests.

My event was a success, I sold all 10 of the pieces I showcased and left with over $5,000 in my pocket. Days like this make me want to stop doubting myself and become an artist full time. After taking a hot shower and eating dinner, Rim and I watched a documentary about our favorite artist, Jacob Lawrence. Our professor from college loved him, so we learned about him during class. Like always Rim fell asleep before it ended so, I went to my art studio to continue working on my painting for Gabby. The card I received from Dean caught my attention. Sitting at my desk, I contemplated opening the blue envelope in my hands. After going back and forth with myself, I ripped opened the envelope and smiled. The card said "Congratulations" with a paintbrush and a palette on the front. When I opened it, a $200 gift card fell out into my lap and I shook my head while smiling. Dean's handwriting caught my attention before the generic card greeting did.

Chubs,

I am so proud of you for showcasing and selling your work. I know all of your pieces are like your babies you never want to let go. Continue to follow your dreams and always, always remain true to yourself. I will still support you whether you want me to or not. ;)

Love,

Dean.

I held the card to my chest as my heart raced. It meant a lot to me knowing that even after I cut him off, he still wanted to support me. I reread the card a few more times before I began painting. I had Kali Uchis' latest album playing in the background. I was so lost in my work I didn't know Rim was standing behind me watching.

"I love watching you in your zone." He walked behind me and put his arms around my waist. His presence threw me off. The whole time I was painting Dean was on my mind. After all, many of the songs on her album I listened to with Dean. While we were dating, we would find new music for one another to listen to. My music taste was more neo-soul/r&b while Dean was a real rap/hip-hop head. During the weeknights, we would lie on the couch and just play music for hours and talk about different artists. Even now I catch myself listening to rappers I never paid any attention to before Dean. Rim started kissing my neck causing me to stiffen up in his arms.

"You're breaking my focus," I said with a light laugh. I slowly moved out of his arms and put my palette down.

"My bad, you just look so good painting in your sports bra and yoga pants." He licked his lips, "I've been waiting damn near seven years to finally have you." We both laughed, mine was more out of being uncomfortable. Although we hadn't had sex yet, Rim has made it very clear that he is ready whenever I am. There have been plenty of times when we could've crossed that line, but I always worried how it would affect our friendship. Even now I think about how it will affect us. Feeling exasperated by the thoughts racing through my mind, I cleaned up before heading to my bedroom and Rim followed behind me.

"Listen, I know it's only been a little over a month, but I feel like we are ready to take the next step. We've been friends for a long time there's no need to continue taking things slow. What you think?" He grabbed my waist making me look him in his eyes.

"I don't know, Rim. I don't want to rush us. Just because we were great as friends doesn't mean we will make a great couple. There are still things I am learning about you and vice versa." I meant that.

In the past, I rushed into relationships, and my last one left me pregnant by a man who was in a whole other relationship while we were together. I had a miscarriage, and he moved on. I knew then I wouldn't rush into anything else. So between that, and my heart missing Dean, I just wanted to be as cautious as possible.

"Ok. I'll give you some time to think about it," Rim said as he dropped his hands from my waist, sighed and shrugged his shoulders. Rim wasn't the type to argue or fight. He was very laid back and sometimes that was *boring*. I watched as he went to the bathroom to shower. After getting settled in bed, I scrolled through my Instagram feed and was humbled at all the pictures I was tagged in. The first thing to catch my eye was my favorite painting "*Moonlight.*" I clicked the notification and was pleasantly surprised to see that Dean was the one who purchased my painting. The caption read "Supporting an old friend." Maybe I should stop giving Dean such a hard time and build a friendship with him. He is still as persistent and consistent as he was a year ago. I put my phone down and laid on my side letting my thoughts consume me as I fell asleep.

"YOUR ART SHOWCASE WAS AMAZING, SIS." Ives beamed. We are at brunch talking about my show, but I still hadn't told her about my conversation with Dean or the sweet card he gave me. We had a lot of catching up to do.

"Thanks, I still can't believe I sold all of my paintings," I said, serenely. "Last night was just what I needed to motivate me." After taking a sip of my mimosa, I took the chance to confront Ivy on Deans attendance. "So Dean was there..." I squinted my eyes at her.

"Whoa, I had nothing to do with that," Ives held her hands up in defense. "Grant told him about the event earlier that day. I think it's sweet that he showed up though. Especially after you cut him off with no explanation," she sipped her orange juice.

"You're one to talk after all the games you put Grant through." We both laughed. "No, but seriously, it was sweet of him to come. He gave me flowers, a gift card and a handwritten card that had the sweetest message." I covered my face to hide that I was blushing. *What is happening to me?*

"Aww. You miss him?" Ivy was smiling from ear to ear. "I don't see why y'all can't work on a friendship. He misses you a lot. I overhear some of the conversations he has with Grant and know that if you called him tomorrow saying you wanted him in your life he would come running, trust me." She went back to eating her omelet.

"I don't know. Having Dean around will only confuse me more," I sighed. "Things with Rim are starting to escalate. He thinks we are moving too slow," I said while cutting my pancake. "But I don't know. Rushing into a relationship is not something I want to do again."

Or maybe being with Rim is something I didn't really want. After only five months with Dean, I knew I wanted to be with him. Today during my run, I found myself listening to the playlist Dean made me last year for Valentine's Day. Listening to the playlist brought back memories, our first date, the weekend we spent in D.C., how every Saturday morning we went to brunch then a museum. We really shared some great times together. Within those five months, we did more than I've done in all my past relationships combined. I was more open with him too for the most part.

"Or maybe you need to stop playing and talk to Dean. Forget Rim, I don't see the chemistry between you two at all." She waved her hand. "I think you are dating him because he's safe. I understand why you ended things with Dean last year but the way he lit up when he saw you at Grant's birthday dinner," she shook her head while smiling. "If you really wanted to be with Rim, you would be with him. We've known him what seven years? You've seen him in relationships you know the type of man he is. You're stalling."

"No, I'm not. I'm cautious," I lied.

Ives giving me the third degree had sweat beads forming on my forehead. I know she isn't the biggest fan of Rim. She made that known the moment she met him. "When did you become so hashtag '*Team Dean?*' You couldn't stand him more than me at one point."

When I told her about him having a baby, she was ready to go to war with him. Now she's vouching for him?

"I got to know him on a different level after Grant and I got married. I understand him a little better after a few heart to hearts we've shared. Don't try and deflect from the original topic," she pointed her fork at me. "What's stopping you from calling Dean just to say thank you for the card?" she tapped her fork on her plate waiting for my response.

I narrowed my eyes at her. "This date was not supposed to turn into this." I guess this is my karma for being so heavily involved in her dating life before Grant.

"Hey, you brought him up. I took it as an opportunity to share my thoughts. I am not saying to run back into his arms, but at least tell him why you cut him off in the first place." She held her hand up, "Before you go off listen, it took me years to talk about my abuse, so I understand you wanting to protect your heart, I really do. I know your miscarriage is still fresh and still hurts. If you aren't ready to talk about that at least tell him about Vaughn. Just so you know, he has asked me numerous times if there are any underlying reasons you cut him off, but I told him that's something he'll have to talk to you about. He understands why you wanted to just be friends, but he feels like you are punishing him for having a child. And you kinda are punishing him, you all weren't together when Yara was conceived. He's not Vaughn..." I jerked my head back at the mention of my ex, Vaughn. Just the mention of him put a bad taste in my mouth.

I cut her off, "I am not punishing Dean. I am protecting myself, ok!" I slammed my fist down on the table. "Ivy, I don't want to talk about this anymore," I said, as I threw my fork down.

Ivy nodded slowly, "Noted."

For the rest of our meal, we ate in silence. Even though we initially rode together, I decided to take the train home. I needed time alone to sort through these thoughts. Almost everything Ivy said was right, *almost*.

I *do* miss Dean.

I *am* dating Rim because he's safe.

I *am* prolonging this courting stage because I'm not all in with him.

But I am not punishing Dean because of Vaughn, that is one thing I will not take accountability for.

When I reached my place, I sent Ivy a message letting her know I made it home safely. She one-worded me "same." Her short response made me shake my head. She is so stubborn. I was the bigger person and apologized for blowing up on her like that. Truthfully, I was wrong. Vaughn is still a sore spot for me. He is a topic I never want to talk about. He occupied too much of my time while in therapy. I spent too many sessions crying over the heartache he caused me. After completing 10 sessions with Dr. Lewis, we both agreed I was making significant progress. But the way I blew up on Ives today had me thinking otherwise. I shouldn't have gotten so angry at her for being honest with me. If she feels as if I am punishing Dean, then maybe I need to lighten up on him. The animosity I have isn't with him.

He didn't cheat on me.

He didn't abandon me while I was grieving.

In no way does he deserve the cold treatment I have been giving him. Dean was the first man I seriously dated after my miscarriage. He was the first man I thought could change my view on love and relationships, but that was shut down before we even started. The rest of my day I went back and forth with myself about how I have been treating Dean.

"*He's not Vaughn*," kept replaying in my mind. For some reason, that really bothered me. Not wanting to repeat the same argument with Ives, I started painting as a quick distraction. After completing a small floral piece, I checked my phone in hopes that Ivy's stubborn self, accepted my apology. I read the simple response from Ivy, "Just call him..."

I sighed, the abrupt ending of Vaughn and I didn't allow me to express my disgust with how he treated me, and how he handled us losing our child. However, I do owe Dean some answers. After scrolling through my contacts for Dean's number, my throat tightened as I pressed call.

5

*D*ean

THE NAME that appeared on my phone changed my whole mood. Work has been stressful today, for the first time I have hosting gigs at both of my New York clubs all weekend. The DJ we scheduled for Saturday night at Linx, double booked us. For the last hour, my assistant has been trying to find another DJ to fill in, but this phone call from Autumn made me quickly forget about the perils of today. Since Autumn's art show she'd been on my mind nonstop.

The conversation we had was so short, but I could feel the uncertainty from her. Autumn didn't know I could read her like the back of my hand. The way our bodies melted into one another when we hugged let me know that she misses me just as much as I miss her. All she has to do is say the words, and we could pick up where we left off. Never have I been this emotionally attached to a woman. Even after a year apart I still crave her in the worst way.

"Ms. Richardson," I answered, smiling uncontrollably.

She chuckled, "Mr. Holmes, how are you?" Hearing her laugh made me relax into my seat.

"Better now that you called. To what do I owe this pleasure?" I rested my phone on my shoulder as I shuffled through the contract my assistant just brought to me. Fortunately, we were able to find a DJ for Saturday.

"I, uh...thank you for the card," she paused. "Does that dinner offer still stand?"

I leaned forward resting my elbows on the desk. "Yes it does. You let me know when and where."

"Ok, tonight 8 pm and you should know where."

"Your favorite soul food spot. How could I forget?" I chuckled. After checking the time, I saw we had a good four hours before our date. "I'll see you then." After I disconnected our call, I leaned back in my seat. I'm not sure what this dinner has in store, but for the first time, Autumn wasn't tense or defensive while speaking to me, I'll take that as a good sign.

The next call I received would instantly ruin my

good mood if answered, my mother. Yesterday when I went to pick up Yaya we had a disagreement about me reaching out to my father. I don't know what has gotten into her lately, what caused her sudden change of heart? She told me now that I am a father I should look at things from his perspective. I'm not trying to hear that. My mother fails to see how their divorce affected me. Yes, I was an adult when it happened, but watching what I viewed as the 'picture perfect' marriage crumble right before me; hurt me to no end. The only person I ever looked up to let me down. As much as my father preached to me about being faithful, how marriage is work, sacrifice, and being selfless when it comes to your spouse. He did the opposite of everything he told me to do. All the bullshit he preached to me just for him to cheat with a girl old enough to be my sister. I would never do anything to risk separation and cause strife in my family. As respectfully as I could, I told my mother that this topic is dead. I have nothing to say to him. After watching her call go to voicemail, I resumed reading over the contract for the DJ we would book for Saturday.

WAITING for Autumn's arrival at the restaurant had my nerves through the roof. Usually, I am nonchalant and unbothered, but Autumn brings out something else in me. She had me doing things I felt were corny, like having a bouquet of flowers in hand. I chuckled at how soft I was becoming, but if that's what I had to do to get her back then so be it. I've wanted to have this time with her for over a year. Whatever I have to do to show that I was appreciative of her time I will do. When she walked into the restaurant, we locked eyes before she looked away. I stood from my seat to embrace her, but she sat down quickly. I was already feeling like this dinner wasn't going to go well, but I shook negative thoughts as I took my seat. While we waiting for the waitress to return with our drinks, I admired the beauty sitting before me. She dressed casually in a pair of distressed jeans, a tank top, and heeled sandals. Her hair was in a big puff with two curls hanging by her ears. Autumn's heart-shaped face was on full display, moles and all. She was breathtakingly beautiful, and she never had to do much.

"I'm glad you had a change of heart," I said as she looked over the menu. There was no need for her to even pick up the menu. We both knew what she was getting. Every time we came here, she ordered smothered chicken, collard greens, and candied yams.

"Yeah, it's time we sat down and talked about everything," she said, never looking up from the menu. After placing our orders with the waitress, I stared at her waiting for her to speak her piece. "I want to apologize for cutting you off the way I did. I handled that a little immaturely," she chuckled. "When I said I want to be friends, I meant it. However, I wasn't sure what that meant for us. Like how do we put aside the feelings we had for each other and be just friends?" She paused. "So, I felt not talking to you at all would make it easier to accept that we can't be together." The genuine sadness in her eyes made my heart sink.

I reached across the table for her hand, "Why can't we be together? Because I have a daughter? That's a deal breaker for you?" I bit my lip as I waited for her response.

"That's not it," she hesitated.

"Then what is it?" I raised my right brow. She removed her hand from my hold.

After taking a moment to think she replied, "I had some things I needed to work on." She broke eye contact with me causing my heart rate to increase.

"Things like what?" I asked eagerly. From the beginning, Autumn was very open with me, or so I thought. She touched on her last boyfriend and how it changed her view of relationships, but she never went into detail. Maybe that's my fault, I should've pushed her to open up. Especially after I was transparent with her about my parents' divorce changing my perception of marriage. Their divorce was strictly off limits, but Autumn made me feel comfortable, like I could trust her more than I've ever trusted any woman.

She exhaled, "Let's just focus on building a

friendship right now, Dean. I can't offer you anything more than that, seriously."

Pinching the bridge of my nose, I said, "Ok." I didn't want to ruin the semi-comfortable vibe we had right now, so I changed the subject. If she only wants to be friends then I will do that, for now. But this time I'm not going to chase her, she will have to put forth the effort first.

We used the rest of dinner to catch up with one another. I told Chubs about the status of YaYa's Place, my new club in L.A. She told me about her next art showcase and how she's preparing. I made her promise to invite me the next time. After getting over the nerves of being around each other, the conversation went smoothly. One topic we never discussed, Yara. I didn't know if she would be open to knowing about my life as a father. Eventually, we will be able to talk about it, but not tonight. Baby steps, I guess. Afterward, I drove her home. We kept the conversation going, I even put her on to some new music. That aspect of our relationship was something I appreciated. When we weren't talking, I would listen to all the music she played while she painted. Listening to music is one of my favorite past times. But listening to music with Autumn was another level of intimacy. Autumn had me telling her stories about how artists or a particular song changed my life. No woman before or after her could make me that vulnerable. Playing new music for one another felt like old times. I caught her smiling a few times as she bobbed her head to the music. It was then I knew she missed this as much as I did. When I pulled up to her place, I put the car in park. I wasn't ready for her to go inside yet or for this night to end.

"Your little boyfriend waiting inside for you?" I asked half-jokingly.

"He's not my boyfriend. Your girlfriend waiting for you to come home?" Autumn shot back. I see relationships is something we will have to keep off limits for now.

With a chuckle, I said, "You know she's not my girl."

"You never know with you," she countered. That's another thing I miss about Autumn, she always has a witty comeback.

"Alright, you got it." I raised my hands in defense. "When will I see you again?" I licked my lips as I waited for her response. A smile appearing before, she quickly dropped it.

"One step at a time, Dean," she said as she opened the car door. I unbuckled my seatbelt to walk her to the door. Once she was inside, Autumn turned to me.

I grabbed her free hand and kissed it, "Thank you for having dinner with me, Chubs."

Autumn bit her lip as she gazed into my eyes. While staring at each other I caressed her hand with my thumb, Autumn cleared her throat, "Good night, Dean."

I cupped her cheek before planting a soft kiss on her forehead, "Night, sweetheart."

Her cheeks rose as a smile appeared on her face and she shook her head as she closed the door. Satisfied with the way our night ended I walked back to my car with a pep in my step. I left feeling like we were on our way to building a friendship, unlike last year. Although I want more, I will work on making that solid foundation to prove to her that we can be together despite me having a child.

"Yaya, don't put that in your mouth," I chastised, while taking the remote from her hands. We were laying in bed watching *Mickey Mouse Clubhouse*, our morning ritual. She started to whine, but that ceased when I shot her my "don't even think about it" glare. She crawled to the end of the bed and sat with her legs crossed. I guess she was sick of me. Yaya reminds me so much of myself it's crazy. She forces me to come face to face with some of my flaws. I laughed at her having an attitude. As much as I wanted to be mad at her, I couldn't. She has me wrapped around her finger.

While we spent our Sunday being lazy, I sent a text Autumn to see what she was doing. The last few weeks we have talked here and there. She was really putting forth the effort for us to have a friendship and

I appreciated that. Often I questioned whether I was thirsty by texting her first, but she responded and kept the conversation going, so I took that as a good sign. I remembered that she spent her Sunday's painting. She usually keeps her phone on '*do not disturb*' while in her zone, so when I saw her face timing me, I was both surprised and eager at the same time.

"Hey, beautiful." I smiled into the camera.

She returned the smile and replied, "Hey, you." I couldn't help but stare at her, she had on a Nike sports bra with her hair in two cornrows. Either she is preparing for her daily run, or about to do yoga.

"What you up to?" I put my arm behind my head.

"Just finished doing yoga. Now, I am about to shower and paint. Why are you still in bed? It's almost noon," she said, still holding a smile.

"Sunday's are my lazy days, remember? I'm chillin' in bed with babygirl."

Autumn's smile lowered. "Oh, if I'm interrupting I can call back."

I quickly cut her off, "No, it's cool. She is mad at me right now." I turned the camera to Yaya still at the end of the bed wholly engrossed in the adventures of Mickey and his crew. When I called her name, she turned around with her arms folded over her chest.

"Aww, she is too cute. What did you do to her?" Autumn said with furrowed brows.

"Why did it have to be me? She was misbehaving," I laughed. "What are you doing later tonight though?"

She looked up like she was really thinking about her plans. "Hmm, lesson plans for the week, why?"

"Maybe I want to come to see you. Haven't seen you since we had dinner." I know I'm pushing it by trying to pull up on her, but I've always been one to push the envelope. Truthfully, I missed her. Autumn has made a permanent space in my mind and heart. Sure we were talking every day, but being in her presence was something I yearned for. Telling Autumn I miss her was on the tip of my tongue, and I had to catch myself.

"Dean," she laughed. "What did I say after dinner?"

"One step at a time? What does that mean, Chubs? Don't friends hang out with one another?" I countered, with a sly smile. The boundaries she is trying to create to ensure we don't cross any lines are starting to frustrate me. I genuinely like being around Autumn, her aura naturally lifts spirits.

"It means, you can't come over my house right now and vice versa. I'm about to start setting up to paint. I'll send you a picture of what I'm working on." I blew out a breath annoyed that she shot me down again.

"Cool, later, Boo." I winked knowing that would make her laugh.

Autumn shook her head before hanging up. Last week she called herself trying to "check" me about calling her Boo. But if I had to comply with these bullshit boundaries, she was putting in place the least she could do was let me call her any term of endearment I wanted. That was my way of compromising.

After spending the day watching cartoons and lying around, Yaya and I headed to my mother's house for Sunday dinner. Surprisingly, since our argument, my mother and I hadn't really talked. I continued my daily check in to see how she is doing. Our conversations lasted five minutes max. Of course, I apologized for my tone and raising my voice at her. I should've never allowed my anger to make me forget who I was talking to. Disrespecting my mother is something I don't take lightly. It had been a while since we got into something this heated. I know that is why she was so adamant about us having dinner tonight.

I entered her house through the side door of the garage. She was in the kitchen finishing up the meal for the evening.

"Hey, Ma," I kissed her on the cheek.

"Silas." She went back to stirring the corn she was frying.

"Come on, ma. You still mad? Why did you invite me over for dinner then?" I asked, my forehead wrinkled in confusion.

"Put Yaya in her high chair," she ordered while making Yaya a plate of vegetables. Reluctantly, I followed her instructions. Afterward, I sat at the dining room table and waited for her next order. I knew not to try her when she was in this mood. She made both our plates and sat across the table from me. Yaya was in the middle of us eating her yams and peas.

"Alright, let me have it," I said, ready for her to go in.

"Silas, you are my only child. I couldn't imagine how it would feel to not speaking to you every day." I looked down. She grabbed my hand, "What if you made a mistake and Yara cut you off for years." I looked at Yaya, and she waved.

"Ma, You don't understand," I mumbled while shaking my head.

"Help me understand how you can cut off someone you were so close with?" My mother leaned back in her chair.

"He hurt you. He hurt us," I said louder than I intended. After taking a deep breath, I continued, "Did you all think about how the divorce may have affected me? My whole world was turned upside down. I saw a side of both of you that I never knew even existed. Do you remember the night you exploded at dinner? The tears that were in your eyes as you cooked dinner? You were so broken emotionally and mentally. And all by the man I admired. The man I wanted to be like let me down in the worst way. Do you know how many nights I sat up listening to you cry from my guest room? How many conversations I overheard from you and Aunt Bee about how broken you felt? And there was no way I could make it better. He single-handedly changed my perception of love and marriage. I can't forgive as easily as you did, Ma, I just can't," I ran my hand over my face, "I am trying to deal with this my own way. Not talking to him is my way for now."

I looked into my mother's eyes; she was fighting to hold back the tears that formed during my rant. This is the first time I was honest with her about why I no longer want a relationship with him.

"Baby," she stood from her seat and pulled me into a hug. "I am so sorry I never considered how our separation affected you." We rocked back and forth as my mother hugged me tightly. "Thank you for sharing this with me. I will back off for now, but I still think you should consider his feelings in all this. Like I said you all were close, and now there's nothing."

I nodded my head, "I'll give it some thought."

6

𝒜 utumn

RIM HAD to go back on tour the day after my art show. After touring two weeks straight, he is home on a three-day break. The last conversation we had about taking things to the next level was the furthest thing from my mind. Honestly, since he left, I hadn't thought about him much. He was still consistent in sending me a daily motivational text message, he called me before, and after a show. Things were still the same, but somehow I felt different. I tried to ignore that my growing friendship with Dean was the reason; which is why I did all I could to keep us strictly in the friend zone. As expected, Dean tried his hardest to push the limits of us being more than friends. Fortunately, I was standing firm in my decision to have some boundaries in place. Those boundaries didn't stop the butterflies I felt when he called or text me. Or the smile that would appear every time he called me, Chubs or Boo.

I looked over the pinstripe jumpsuit I chose to wear to the open mic night Rim and I are going to tonight. *You look bomb.* I winked at my reflection. Since the weather has cooled down, I went to the Dominicans for a blowout. My kinky curls were now straight with a middle part, my favorite fall look. After touching up my makeup, I was ready to head out the door. I paired the jumpsuit with a pair of red heels and minimal jewelry. To keep it simple I wore my signature nameplate necklace and diamond earrings, the last birthday gift I received from my mother. Like clockwork, Dean facetimed me like he knew I was about to go out.

"Hey, Boo. Where are you going?" he smiled into the camera. I bit my bottom lip to hide my growing smile.

"Out," I merely said.

"Oh, you have a date with your little boyfriend?"

Rolling my eyes, I responded, "Yes."

Dean's eyes widened. "So he is your boyfriend?" he kept his eyes on me, but I saw the sadness in them. A part of me felt bad, but we aren't together, so I quickly straightened up.

"Dean, I don't have time for this right now. I'm running late."

"Aight, Autumn," he disconnected the call. Shaking my head while laughing, seeing Dean jealous was cute. After turning off the lamp in my room, I walked downstairs to meet Rim.

"You look amazing, babe," Rim said as he hugged me.

"Thanks," I said, while trying to move from his tight hold. I needed to get it together and figure out this weird feeling. No matter how close Dean and I are becoming I can't let that mess up the thing I have going with Rim. Rim kissed my temple as we walked out the door.

"I missed you so much," he whispered in my ear.

My throat went dry, "I missed you too."

After we arrived at Milk & Honey Cafe', we found a table off to the right of the stage. We were regulars here so when our waitress came to the table she already had my green tea with honey and Rim's blueberry hibiscus tea in hand. We thanked her before turning our attention back to the performer. She was doing an acoustic version of H.E.R's song *Every Kind of Way*. Rim rested his arm around my shoulder as he pulled me closer to him, I looked up at him and smiled. I knew this was low-key our song. For our first official date, we went to see H.E.R. and ever since then her self-titled album was *ours*. After her set ended, I excused myself to go to the restroom to freshen up. I leaned against the stall door and checked my phone in hopes that I received a text or call from Dean.

What are you doing? I asked myself after I saw he hadn't done either. I am out with one man while thinking about the other, this isn't me at all. After washing my hands, I returned back to my date with Rim. Whatever I was or wasn't feeling I needed to figure it out quick.

WHILE GETTING ready for my morning run, I received a call from Ivy that put me in a panic. As soon as I answered the phone, she burst into tears.

"Ives, what's wrong? Is Gabby ok? Did something happen to Grant?" Every possible scenario that would lead her to call me crying played in my head.

"It's Ms. Pam," Ivy sobbed in my ear. "Last night she was robbed at gunpoint then shot. It-it's really bad, sis." Ivy put the phone down and began crying. Grant took the phone and continued to tell me what happened. All I could think about is how Dean is handling all of this. Ms. Pam is his world.

"I am so sorry this happened to her," I said, unsure of what else to say.

"Me too. We went to the hospital last night, and it was bad. She was rushed into emergency surgery for her gunshot wound. We are waiting to hear back from the doctor. You should call Dean," Grant suggested.

"I will call him later today."

"Thanks, fam." I heard Gabby crying in the background. "I have to go. Ivy will call you later." Grant ended the call.

My workday felt like it would never end, I found myself staring at the clock waiting for it to be 4 pm. When I finally got home, I dropped my bags at the door and began undressing on my way to my bedroom. I sat down on my bed and laid back. After dialing Dean's number, I stared at it for what felt like an eternity. He occupied my mind most of the day. That had become my norm since he came back into my life. Since my date with Rim, our communication had come to an abrupt stop. I knew the reason was me saying Rim is my boyfriend which isn't true. I blew out a breath as I pressed call. The phone rang three times before he answered.

"Hello?" His voice so soothing, as always.

"Hey, Dean it's Autumn." I smacked my forehead. *Why wouldn't he know who it is?*

"I know who it is," he chuckled.

"Right. I heard about your mother, and I just wanted to call and check on you." I bit my bottom lip. There was a brief pause before he answered. I heard him sigh.

"I'm good," he said in a stern tone.

"You sure? You can talk to me," I rolled onto my stomach. He was short with me, that wasn't a good sign.

"Yea. I'm sure. I have to go, will talk to you later."

He hung up. I stared at my phone screen for a few seconds. I wanted to call back, but I felt like the call wasn't enough. I jumped up, threw some clothes on and hopped in my car with every intention of going to his house.

Standing at his front door, I contemplated whether I should turn around and go back home. After he hung up on me last week, we hadn't spoken at all. I figured he was being typical stubborn Dean. Then I remembered the hurt in his voice today and how his mother is the most important person in his life. Whatever issue he has with me seeing Rim will have to be put on the back burner for now and I need to be there as his friend. After ringing the doorbell, I stood anxiously waiting for him to answer. When Dean answered, he looked surprised to see me on his front doorstep. For a moment we stood in silence staring deeply into each other's eyes. His piercing stare became too intense, so I broke the silence.

"I wanted to come to check on you because a phone call wasn't enough. Can I come in?" I waited for him to move to the side so I could come in. He was still quiet which was unlike him, but I know he has a lot going on both mentally and emotionally. We sat on his couch and I took a moment to look him over. His hair was unbrushed, he hadn't shaved, and he had on joggers and no shirt, yet he still looked so good in my eyes. I grabbed his hand and looked into his sad eyes.

"How are you? Like really? You can be honest with

me. I was in your shoes a few years ago." I rubbed his hand softly as I waited for his response. He took his free hand and ran it over his face before answering.

"I don't know, Chubs. It's just a lot to try to process. Just last week we were arguing about me fixing my relationship with my father. Now she's laying in a hospital bed." He hung his head down and his shoulders slumped. "How am I supposed to feel?"

When he looked back up, I saw the gloss over his eyes. I pulled him into a hug. He rested his head on my shoulder as I rubbed his back in circular motions. I was all too familiar with this hurt. Knowing you could lose your loved one at any moment, it's a terrible feeling, and I wouldn't wish it on anyone. When my mother was diagnosed with heart disease, my world came tumbling down. On top of that, she refused to change her diet and take her prescriptions which ultimately led to her having a heart attack. The thought of how emotionally draining her death made me had tears forming in my eyes. We sat in silence as I held him in my arms. I had so many questions I wanted to ask about his mother's condition, but I knew that Dean had been trying to keep it together. One thing I learned about him is he will never let you see him sweat.

"I appreciate you coming to check on me. I miss you. I miss us. This friendship shit we are trying to do. It doesn't feel right." Dean massaged his temples. I tensed up and removed my arms from around him. This isn't a conversation I wanted to have.

"We don't need to talk about that Dean...really. This isn't the time," I said waving my hand.

"No, this is the time," He grabbed my arm. "I need you to know that us not being together eats at me every day. I'm trying to accept that we can only be friends right now. I know me being a first-time father while we were trying to build our relationship wasn't ideal." He shook his head, "I don't know I just wish things could've gone differently. I lost my best friend."

He wasn't the only one who lost his best friend. I had been suffering too. Dean had apologized a million times via calls, texts, and even when we had dinner. Yet somehow this time it just felt different. Maybe it was seeing him visibly hurt by from us not being together and knowing his mother is in a coma it made my cold demeanor breakdown.

"It wasn't all you," I sighed. "I was in the midst of getting over past hurt. Finding out about you having a baby on the way only magnified the demons I was running from. I shouldn't have shut you out so abruptly. Again, I apologize." I pushed a loose strand of hair behind my ear before looking Dean in the eye after finally admitting why I ended things so suddenly.

"Whatever you were going through I would've helped you get through it," he said, firmly. If only he knew that I was recovering from a miscarriage and being on a love high with him helped numb me from the pain. The day I heard Liliana tell him she's pregnant, my stomach dropped, and the high I was on came to an end. Reality quickly punched me in the face reminding me that the possibility of being a mother was faint and that type of baggage would've caused more damage than good to our relationship. "Do you miss me?" When he asked I looked back down. He grabbed my chin making me look him in the eye again. Of course, I miss him. I cut off someone I talked to every day for five months straight. Dean had quickly become part of my daily routine. We clicked in a way that I knew didn't happen every day. That's why I am having a hard time trying to keep this friendship strictly platonic. No matter how I tried to fight my resurfacing feelings for him I knew deep down I wanted him back.

It took me a few days to come to that realization regarding Dean, but since I was being honest with myself, I also had to admit that Rim and I weren't meant to be anything but friends. Dean is who I want to be with. Dean waited for my answer, he stared intensely into my eyes. I felt weak under his watch and I wasn't a good liar, so it was no point in me lying to him.

Without thinking twice and because I missed him more than he knew, I responded, "yes." Before I could get it out good, his lips were against mine. He leaned back allowing me to lie on top of him as we continued to kiss. The feel of his hands roaming freely up and down my body had me removing my shirt so I could feel his touch against my bare skin. He helped me pull my shirt over my head before throwing it on the floor. Next, he unhooked my bra. He bit his bottom lip as he sat up while holding me so I wouldn't fall off his lap. Dean kissed my neck and chest hungrily as he pulled my hair out of the bun it was in. As much as I wanted to prevent this from happening, it felt so damn good.

"I missed you so much," he whispered in my ear before continuing to nibble on it causing chills down my spine. This man had my body under his spell again.

"I-I missed you too," I moaned. He picked me up and carried us upstairs to his bedroom. He made sure to never stop kissing me.

As our tongues collided with one another, Dean laid me down gently on the bed making sure we never disconnected from our kiss. I don't know when he took off both of our pants, but the feel of him at my opening had the seat of my panties getting wetter than they already were.

"She's ready for me," he said against my lips. I nodded my head and wrapped my legs around his waist to pull him closer to me. He tugged at my waist waiting for me to unwrap my legs around him. He took my panties off and slowly slid inside my honeypot. Dean groaned in my ear as he continued to inch inside of me. I know he felt my body tensing up because he whispered, "relax." He took my hands and pulled them over my head. His strokes sped up, and he never took his eyes off me as he continued to make love to my body. With every moan he released, I felt myself getting wetter and weaker.

"I'm sorry for hurting you, baby? Do you believe me?" He asked as he slowed his strokes down. I was in a state of euphoria. My stomach muscles tightened at the same time my legs started to shake.

"Yes," I yelled out as I let my orgasm take over my body.

"I'll never hurt you again, Autumn," he whispered in my ear before kissing it. In my heart, I knew he would never hurt me again. He hooked my legs over his arms and slowly entered me inch by inch causing me to become completely unhinged. Dean leaned down and took my bottom lip into his mouth as he reached his peak. We both laid there caressing one another. I snuggled under his arm, and we fell asleep.

The next morning I woke up to an empty bed, I ran to the bathroom to wash my face and brush my teeth. Luckily, I remembered where Dean kept spare toiletries. I put on his t-shirt and slowly walked downstairs. As I entered his living room, I heard him on the phone. Judging by the topic, Yara, I'm assuming he is on the phone with Liliana. I really can't have any ill feelings towards her, especially if I am going to continue to be friends with Dean. I continued past him to his kitchen to pour a cup of orange juice while he wrapped up his call.

"Morning, beautiful," Dean whispered, as he kissed my neck. I couldn't help but smile as he wrapped his arms around my waist.

"Good morning." Turning around in his arms I asked, "How are you?" I cupped his cheek as I looked into his eyes for any sign of sadness.

"I'm fine," he said as he loosened his grip around my waist.

Grabbing his hands before he stepped back I said, "Don't shut down on me."

He sighed. "Can we just enjoy this?" he pointed between us. "That's all I want to do right now, Chubs. I have to make sure everything is straight with my clubs for tonight and check on my mother. Let me enjoy having you to myself, please."

"Ok, fine."

Not wanting to start an argument I decided to make us breakfast. Dean's fridge was stocked with all the ingredients needed to make my favorite, huevos rancheros. After a peaceful meal, I put on my clothes from yesterday to go home. Dean walked me to my car and opened the door for me. He kissed my temple as I slid into the driver's seat.

"I don't want last night to cause any confusion between us," I said, unsure of how he would feel about me still keeping some type of boundaries in place.

He leaned down, "Yeah, I know *just friends.*" The emphasis he used made me chuckle.

"I'll call to check on you later. Ms. Pam is in my prayers." Dean stepped away from the car after he gave me a slight nod. I had been praying nonstop for Ms. Pam's recovery. I know the chances of her recovering from her wounds are slim, but I still feel like there is still a chance she can pull through.

During my shower, I dissected the events leading up to me sleeping with Dean. We were both caught up in the moment, extremely vulnerable. I knew the only way I could release this mix of feelings is by painting. The sounds of Sade's *Is It a Crime* playing in the background explained how I felt to a tee.

This may come as a surprise
But I still want you…

My paintbrush became my microphone as I belted out the chorus, the words to this song were everything I needed to say to Dean and more.

Is it a crime
That I still want you
And I want you to want me too.

Hours later, I stepped back to look over my work. When I first started this, I had no idea where it was going. For the first time in a while, I completely free-styled this piece. Unknowingly, I painted a couple holding one another, the woman is resting her head against her man's chest as he rests his chin on top of her head. Staring at this painting, I knew in my heart what I needed to do. I reached for my phone to make the call I've been dreading all day.

"Rim, we need to talk."

7

D ean

STARING at my mother as she lay hooked up to countless machines crushed me. The person who did this to my mother has to pay, and sadly I know that day may never come. The police report said that she was leaving a restaurant when she was robbed and shot. Unfortunately, the detectives working the case doesn't have any updates as the witness didn't have much to offer. In her defense, she couldn't see much from the building across the street where she resides, besides the shooter being dressed in all black. The witness also said she saw my mother hugging a man before returning to her car.

If my mother was dating someone, I think she

would've told me? I've been racking my brain trying to make sense of everything. Deep down I know they will not find the person responsible. *What was she doing out that late, anyway? Who was the man she was with? If she was dating him, why hasn't he come forward?* The events that led up to my mother being hospitalized kept replaying in my head. We'd spoken that day multiple times, not once did she mention having dinner with someone. The questions that filled my mental could only be answered by one person, and she is currently on life support.

I can't eat.

I can't focus on work.

I am completely restless.

Last week they did emergency surgery to remove the bullet from her head and try to repair her fractured jaw. The injuries she sustained from the shot lets police know that the assailant shot her from close range. She was unconscious when she arrived at the hospital last night due to her substantial blood loss. I was well aware that victims of gunshot wounds to the head had a slim chance of survival, but my mother has to pull through. The surgeon was successful in removing the bullet without causing any further damage. However, with the severity of her wound and the extensive blood loss, she was placed on life support with her team of doctors monitoring her carefully in the coming weeks.

I had no idea what questions to ask or how to handle

any of this, but thankfully, my Aunt Bee has been here never leaving my mother's side. Right now it was just her and me in the room. Growing up Aunt Bee was like a second mother that's how close we are. During my rebellious adolescent years, she was the first person I went to for advice because I knew I could get an honest opinion from her. And most importantly, whatever I told her stayed between us. I've always appreciated how serious Aunt Bee took our bond.

My mother always said they had the wrong children, Aunt Bee should've been my mother, and my mother should've been Grant's. If ever I did something against my mother's standards she would always say *"You are just like your Aunt Bee. Don't listen to nobody but yourself!"* A chuckle escaped me as I wiped away a tear that had fallen.

The wave of sadness that overcame me had me checking the time on my phone. Some fresh air is needed, my thoughts are becoming too much and looking at my mother and Aunt Bee is making me feel worse.

"Where you going, baby?" Aunt Bee asked, snapping out of her zombie-like state.

Running my hand over my face, I sighed. "Need some fresh air. You want something from the cafeteria or vending machine?"

She shook her head. "No, baby I'm fine."

I nodded before opening the door. The person on the

other side was the last person I ever wanted to see, my father.

"What are you doing here?" I gritted. Aunt Bee quickly stood and rushed over to us. She stood in between us with her hand on my chest. "Calm down, baby I told him what happened."

My brows wrinkled as I looked at them both utterly speechless at him being here and Aunt Bee defending his presence. After blowing out a sharp breath, I brushed past them and stormed out the door. "He's not ready yet." I heard my aunt whisper before the door closed.

What the fuck is he doing here? I paced the lobby for five minutes trying to calm myself down. "I have to get out of here," I said aloud. After putting my keys in the ignition, I thought where the hell I would even go? There was no reason for me to go home all I would do is lie awake with my mind and heart racing all night. Scrolling through my contacts I thought about calling Grant, but I know he may be busy. So I called the next best person, Autumn. The night we shared changed a lot for me, I meant every word of me missing her and never hurting her again. All I needed was for her to open her heart to the possibility of giving us another chance.

"Hello?" she answered half asleep. "Is everything ok?" she asked sounding more alert.

"No," I said defeated.

"Did something happen with Ms. Pam?" she asked in a panic.

I sighed, "Nope, still on life support."

"Ok, so what's wrong?"

"My father showed up," I said, resting my head on the back of my seat.

"Dean, I hope you didn't act a fool in that hospital," she hissed.

A laugh came out before I could stop myself. "No, man. I left and called you."

"Good." I heard the smile in her voice. "How much longer are you going to be at the hospital tonight?"

"I'm not sure. Only one person can stay overnight though. Maybe I'll take Aunt Bee up on her offer to go home."

"You are more than welcome to come here."

My eyebrows shot up. "For real?" Autumn hadn't invited me over since we started talking again. That was the first boundary she put in place.

She laughed. "Yes. I will not let you go home and sulk."

"Ok, I'll be there in an hour tops." After disconnecting the call, I thought about going back to tell my Aunt Bee my plans for the night, but the thought of my father still being in the room made my blood boil. So, I shot her a text letting her know I would return in the morning.

Autumn opened the door in a sports bra and yoga shorts. Her hair was up in a pineapple with a scarf wrapped around it. I felt the need to grab her and kiss her, but I didn't want to ruin the chances of spending the night with her. She turned me on without any effort. *Damn.* I licked my lips pleased with the sight before me.

She grabbed my hand before I stepped through the threshold.

"You good?" she asked, with a look of genuine concern in her eyes.

"I am now," I said before kissing her forehead. Autumn bit her lip to hide that I had her blushing, I remembered how much she loved forehead kisses. She held my hand as she led us to her living room that was dimly lit by various aromatherapy candles. In the middle of the floor was a blanket and two huge pillows with popcorn, wine, and chocolate candy.

Smiling wide I asked, "What's all this, Boo?"

She shrugged. "I figured we would have a movie night to help take your mind off things."

No longer fighting the urge, I grabbed her by her face and kissed her. My kisses started off soft and light, then my need for her her increased, so I started kissing her hard and passionately. She wrapped her arms around my shoulders pulling me closer. I grabbed her legs and picked her up. As our tongues continued to attack one another, I walked us over to the setup she prepared for me.

A moaned escaped Autumn's lips making my need for her urgent. Movie night would have to be rescheduled because I have something else in mind for us. I gripped her soft, round ass as she ground against me. In a split second, Autumn came back to her senses and released her legs from around my waist. I held on tightly to her waist not wanting her to think this was a mistake.

"Dean," she whined and took a step back while shaking her head. "This isn't what I wanted to do tonight."

I exhaled. "Ok let's watch a movie like you planned." Honestly, I'm ok with us not having sex, I enjoy just being in her company. We could've done yoga, and it would still satisfy me. She smiled before grabbing the remote and scrolling through Netflix for a movie for us to watch. After a tough fight between a rom-com and an action film, we decided on our mutual favorite *Inside Man*.

I'm a huge Spike Lee fan, so I am satisfied, and anything with Denzel makes Autumn happy. I sat with my back to Autumn's couch as she leaned under my arm. Tonight with Autumn is a perfect distraction from the emotionally draining days I've been having.

"I like this," I whispered in her ear.

She sat up and faced me. "Me too."

"Chubs, what are we doing?" I asked frustrated by how hot and cold she's been.

"I-," she paused and looked away.

"Do you want to be with me?" I grabbed her hand making her lock eyes with me.

"I do but..."

"But what, Boo?" I looked into her eyes anxiously. "You still messing with ole boy?"

"No," she answered quickly. "I didn't feel like Rim and I are meant to be," she said just above a whisper.

Pleased with her answer, I relaxed,."So why are you forcing this friend thing on us?" I folded my arms waiting for a definite answer. "And saying 'I don't know' isn't acceptable."

Autumn sat on her knees facing me. "The night you called me before my date with Rim, I had been doing a lot of thinking about us, about him, and about what I want." I nodded listening to her attentively. "The days and nights we spent talking on the phone and just genuinely being friends meant a lot to me, I needed that. My last relationship was so rushed, Vaughn came into my life and boom we were in a relationship. No dating, no getting to know each other outside of sex, we just woke up one day and were in a relationship. Well, what I thought was a relationship."

There was a glimmer of sadness in her eyes, but after taking a deep breath, she continued, "I didn't take the time to build that friendship with him. If I did I maybe I would've seen all the red flags before giving my heart and body to him."

"But we had a friendship before you cut me off," I interrupted her.

She shook her head, "No, we were halfway in a

relationship, Dean. I was already falling for you." I smiled, but my smile dropped when she continued. "And that's where I messed up. We needed more time to know each other as friends before we became intimate. Now with Rim, I felt we would work because we have been friends for over seven years. We are great friends, but there was no real chemistry outside of that, and we aren't compatible romantically. With you," she paused and smiled. "It's the best of both worlds, and I was trying to fight it, but I can't. When we didn't speak for a week I was sick. Every day I look forward to talking to you because you are apart of my routine. You are my first thoughts when I wake, and the last before sleep I fall asleep. In just the short month we've been back in each other lives you, have managed to steal my heart and have me gone, yet again. I said all that to say I want to be with you, but I think we should continue to take our time."

I took a few minutes to think over everything Autumn just shared with me. Hearing that she does want to give us another chance made me feel better and was the validation I needed to continue putting in the work to win her over.

Grabbing her chin, I placed a gentle kiss on her lips. "Ok, we can do that." She nuzzled back under my arm, and we finished the movie.

AFTER A WEEK UNDER CLOSE OBSERVATION, my mother still hadn't made any significant progress, but the doctors still wanted to keep a close eye on her. Since then I have been trying to get myself back into my daily routine minus my regular phone calls with her. Aunt Bee told me there is no point in the both of us sitting in the hospital 24/7 and told me to return to work. I have a very trustworthy staff, so I am sure my clubs ran smoothly in my absence. My assistant managers called me in case of emergencies which wasn't often. So imagine my surprise when I received a call about one of my bottle girls, Shay. She was late twice last week and didn't bother showing up at all on Saturday, which tends to be our busiest night.

Don, my assistant manager for Linx, wanted to fire her on the spot, but I pulled rank and told him I would have a meeting with her. Shay has been working for us for three years and never missed a shift. This isn't normal behavior for her, so I figured a conversation would help us all understand what the issue is.

"Hey, boss you wanted to see me?" Shay peeked her head into my office.

"Yes, have a seat," I pointed to the chair in front of my desk. Shay is a 22-year-old college senior. As far as I knew she was in school to get her bachelor's degree in chemistry. During one of the few personal conversations we've had, Shay told me this is her third job... she works on campus and at a clothing store. Even with all that she didn't miss a day of work the entire time she has been here.

"Don mentioned that you were late on Thursday and Friday and didn't even bother showing up on Saturday. He wanted to fire you," I said casually.

"Let me explain," she said nervously, "My ex and the father of my son left me last week. I had to move back in with my mother, and she wasn't able to watch my son, Mason. I should've called, text, something. But this job was the last thing on my mind at the time."

Seeing tears on the brim of her eyes softened my heart. "Don't cry, I figured you had personal issues going on which is why I wanted to sit down and talk."

Becoming a father has made me more sympathetic to other parents. A year ago I would've fired her without hesitation, but I know if I didn't have Liliana and our mothers we could be in the same predicament. The thought of not having my mother to call to watch Yaya at the last minute caused a lump to form in my throat. I swallowed before continuing, "Next time you run into a problem, please contact us. We can't help you if you don't communicate."

She nodded eagerly, "You got it, and I'm sorry."

"It's cool. Don't let it happen again," I said while pointing at her. Shay left out of my office and left the door open for Grant to come in. I hadn't seen him since the night my mother was rushed to the hospital. He called me frequently which is appreciated and other times annoying. During the process of my parent's divorce, I shut everyone out. Grant and I fell off for almost a year during that time. It was nothing against him I was having a hard time coming to terms with everything. After my parent's divorce, he was very clingy whenever tragedies happened. With that in mind, I didn't take it personally when he called multiple times questioning my mental and emotional state; after all, that's what brothers are for, right?

"How are you holding up, bro?" G took a seat.

"I'm maintaining," I stated calmly. Outside of my mother being on life support, I was doing ok. "How about you? How are Ives and Gabby?"

"We are good," he smiled. "I'm surprising Ives with a trip next week. She deserves it. Shit, I deserve it too, but seeing her with Gabby brings about a feeling I never knew existed." The smile on his face is one I've never seen before. I nodded and made a mental note to spend more time at the hospital while Aunt Bee keeps Gabby.

"I had a talk with Autumn the other day…about us," I said while leaning back in my office chair.

"I'm listening," Grant said, resting his chin between his index finger and thumb.

"She said she wants us to continue to build our friendship because she rushed into her last relationship. What do you know about her ex?" I asked.

"I just know they weren't together long, maybe five months max and he cheated on her."

"Interesting. Well, Autumn said she wants to be with me but doesn't want to rush it."

"How do you feel about that?" Grant sat up straight.

I shrugged, "I feel like we'll be together soon. But I get why she wants us to take our time."

Grant smile proudly, "You're finally getting it."

"Huh?" My brows furrowed in confusion.

"You're learning it's not all about what you want. Don't act like you don't know how selfish you can sometimes be, Autumn's needs are equally important. That's how I know she is the one for you. Don't mess this up, bro."

"I won't," I said, firmly. Autumn is everything I want and need in a woman. I'd do anything to make sure she doesn't become 'the one that got away.' Whatever it takes to get and keep her I will do.

"Promise me one thing, bro?" Grant said as he tapped his hands on the armrest.

"Don't shut down on her or me. I know how you get when shit becomes too much to handle. When you grieve, you like to shut everyone out and it's not healthy. If you shut down on Autumn, you will lose her for good." I knew he would bring up how I acted during my parent's divorce, but I took heed to everything he said because if I do lose my mom, Grant and Autumn will be the people I will need to lean on the most.

"I hear you, G."

8

*A*utumn

DURING MY *SHORT* PLANNING PERIOD, I looked at spaces for a potential art studio. Granted, I've done this a million times before, but this time I am serious. The school district I work for is going through budget cuts and guess what programs are getting cut next year? Music and art. Next school year, 15 teachers will be without a job and students will no longer be offered a chance to explore their artistic talents. This was the push I needed to get off my ass and take a leap of faith. My favorite student, Rayna came in and interrupted my search.

"Ms. Richardson, can I come in?" she asked, from the doorway.

"Of course." I motioned for her to come to my desk while closing my laptop to give her my undivided attention. "What's up, lovebug?"

"I decided to apply to NYU Tisch School of the Arts. I finished my admissions essay, and I was wondering if you could look over it for me? Also, I printed out the teacher evaluation form for you to complete."

I smiled as I took the folder that held all the documents. "I am very proud of you, Rayna. I remember you being unsure of what career you wanted to pursue."

"No, Ms. Richardson it was all you. Thank you for pushing me to see how talented I am. If it weren't for you, I would be getting a degree in biology," she laughed. "Which wouldn't have been a bad thing, but I love art more. With the program I am applying to I can combine biology and art which is a happy medium for my parents and myself."

"Good. I know you have a bright future ahead of you no matter what route you take. Although I prefer you to follow your passion. Have you thought about what you want to put in your portfolio?"

She frowned and whispered, "No, I will need your help with building a solid portfolio."

"No worries. Come back tomorrow during my planning period, and we will talk." Rayna's face lit up.

She had the same fire I had when I was her age. My only regret is I didn't have a close relationship with my teacher's like I do with her. If I had the extra push and encouragement from a mentor, I wouldn't second guess myself so much. Like Rayna's parents, my mother wanted me to pursue a career in STEM. However, I knew I wouldn't be happy going that route, so I received a degree in Art & Design and to please my mother, I double majored in marketing. By no means did I think I would be teaching seven years later. But I know there is a reason why I fell into this career, and it's to help my students see their potential. That's why I strive to build trust with every student I come across. Over the years, I have encouraged many of my students to follow their passion and pursue a career in the arts. That was the motivation for me to go to work every day despite all the funding problems I have encountered over the years, but this chapter is coming to a close. Next fall I will be an owner of a thriving art gallery.

After looking at spaces online, I decided on the four I thought matched my vision best. I asked Dean to come with me because he would be able to help me decide. He owns three clubs he knows all about purchasing commercial properties, what square footage I would need, and honestly, I liked having him around. We are still taking things slow, as slow as Dean would allow.

We went on dates and spent a lot of time together, but I felt different this time around. I wasn't clinging on to him to distract me from the loss of my baby, now I'm with him because this is what I want.

Dean has shown a lot of growth as well. The first go-round he was more 'my way or the highway' and I would follow because I needed him. Just like in past relationships, I followed whatever my man said, and I was always left trying to piece my heart back together. I wouldn't consider myself a pushover, no actually, I was a pushover. But I have definitely found my voice, and I am not afraid to use it. Thank God for growth.

The first places we visited were ok, there was nothing spectacular about them. The vision I had for myself didn't work well in the other three sites. Now at the fourth and final place for today, I felt much better about this place. The outside already held my attention. The windows were tall and allowed natural light to shine inside, it helped that this space was on a corner lot at a busy intersection. My mind was already racing with ideas to attract pedestrians.

"What do you think about this place, Chubs?" Dean tugged my hand. I looked around nodding in approval. This space was literally perfect. It was big enough to hold art, and there was a wall separating the front which I would make a reception area. There was enough wall space to hang art and floor space for sculptures. And finally, a corner where I could build a stage for open mic nights could seat about 50 people if set up properly. I spun around one final time smiling from ear to ear.

"I love it." I went on to tell Dean my vision for how everything would be set up and color schemes. Next, I would need to go to the back and apply for a loan. A few months ago I was pre-approved for a loan, but I punked out. Luckily, I kept the card for the loan officer that assisted me.

"Proud of you, Chubs." Dean grabbed my waist and kissed my forehead. "Get the information about this space from the realtor so we can look over it tonight."

"We?" I asked, before biting my lip.

"Yes, you didn't think I was going to watch you sign a lease without myself and a lawyer looking over it first?" he laughed.

"I don't know what I was expecting. I guess I just wanted moral support," I said with a shrug. After we left the last space, we went back to Dean's place. We were both in a great mood and Dean tried convincing me to come to his club tonight to celebrate finding a potential location for my studio. The thought of a night out did sound enticing, but with Ivy and Grant on vacation, I didn't have anyone to party with since he'd be working. Dean assured me I wouldn't feel awkward being there alone. Still, I declined and chose to stay in and binge watch *How to Get Away With Murder*.

When I woke up the next morning Dean's arms were holding me so tight I could barely move. "Don't leave," he whispered in my ear. He kissed my ear and neck and I melted inside. I checked the time, by now I would be out the door for my three-mile run, but I guess I can do it later today.

"What are your plans for the day?" I asked, settling back into his embrace.

"Taking Yara to the park, shopping, and visiting my mother. Want to come with me?" I tensed up causing him to loosen his hold on me. The thought of meeting his daughter made me anxious.

"We aren't officially together yet. I think we should hold off on me meeting Yara."

"Ok, Autumn," Dean mumbled. His response made me even more anxious.

"I will come to the hospital with you though."

"Nah, it's cool. I'm staying overnight." Dean turned to lay on his back.

"Ok," I whispered, feeling the growing tension between us, so I changed the subject. "I'm going to the bank next week to apply for a loan." Dean grunted and sat on the edge of the bed. I rested my head on my right arm waiting for his response, he said nothing. He proceeded to get ready for his day. I'm not sure what caused the shift of energy between us, but I am about to find out. While Dean was in the shower, I sat on the toilet seat. "What's your problem?" I crossed my legs.

Dean poked his head outside the shower curtain and

laughed, "I think you know the answer to that already."
He then went back to washing.

"You don't think it's too soon for me to meet Yara?"
I asked nervously.

"No, but obviously you do." He turned off the water.
I handed him the towel in my lap.

"I mean, yeah, " I shrugged.

"Have you forgiven me for the way you found
about her?"

"Yes," I whispered.

"Why are you uncomfortable every time I bring her
up then?" he looked in the mirror to see my reaction.
"You don't think I sense your uneasiness?" I lowered
my head in shame. I was trying my best not to show
how awkward I felt when Yara is mentioned.

"You remember when I said I had something I was
working to get over?"

Dean put toothpaste on his toothbrush before
answering, "Yes."

"Well, before we met I had a miscarriage," I
murmured, before looking down. I looked back up to
see Dean stopped brushing his teeth. He rinsed out his
mouth before turning to me. He kneeled down in front
of me and grabbed my hands.

"Why didn't you tell me?" he stood and pulled me
into a hug.

"I wasn't ready to talk about it yet," I said, with my
head laying on his bare chest.

He nodded, "Ok. You ready to talk about it now?"

I swallowed the lump in my throat before answering, "Yes." Dean took my hand led us back to his room, and we sat at the end of the bed. He stared at the side of my face as I looked straight ahead. I knew I would have to have this conversation with him one day, but I didn't expect it to be this soon.

"I lost my baby boy when I was four months along. We just found out the gender a few days before." Dean rubbed my knee. "My doctor said I had an incompetent cervix," I chuckled. "But during my grieving process, I learned Vaughn had a whole other relationship. Turns out they had been together for years, and I was introduced into his life while they were on a 'break,' but somewhere down the line they got back together and he never told me. His then-fiancée came to me as a woman and told me to let it go. To let him go. He didn't even have the decency to tell me himself. So yeah, he abandoned me while I was grieving the loss of our child and he'd moved on with a new family."

"And when you found out about Liliana being pregnant it brought back all the hurt you felt?" Dean said nodding his head.

"Yup, I wasn't fully over losing my son, and I couldn't continue dating you. I would be insecure that you would want to work things out with her and I didn't want her to feel like I am trying to keep you from your parental duties." I exhaled, "But last summer I was able to go to therapy and get the help I needed to get over that chapter of my life."

"That's why you stopped talking to me," he said more to himself than to me.

I leaned on his shoulder, "It was more about the pain I was running from like I told you before. You came into my life at a time where I was broken in more ways than one. You were a much-needed distraction." I ran my hand down his chest as I continued, "I do want to meet Yara and eventually talk to Liliana, but let's wait until we get our relationship together."

Dean sat thinking over everything I said. I bit my bottom lip anxiously awaiting his thoughts on everything I had to say. This conversation was needed even if I wasn't completely ready. It isn't fair for him to think I won't be able to accept his daughter because that's not the case at all.

"Now that I know the reasoning behind you cutting me off, I agree with waiting to introduce you and Yara." Dean went to his closet to get dressed. I stood in the doorway watching him sort through his many Nike tech sweatsuits he had hanging up.

"Are we good?" I asked with my heart pounding in my chest. I'm not used to this calm version of Dean. He's never been one to mask his emotions, I didn't want him to blow up on me, but I was expecting something.

He smiled as he walked over to me. Dean kissed me softly on my lips, my cheek, my nose and finally my forehead. "Of course," he said while cupping my cheek. "Thank you for telling me the truth."

I kissed his palm and smiled. Finally, I felt like we were on the same page about everything.

"ALRIGHT MS. RICHARDSON, you are approved for $20,000," said Mr. Woodson, the loan officer.

"A few months ago I was approved for twice as much," I said with furrowed brows. "Why did it decrease?"

"There was a change in your credit score, Ma'am," he stated calmly.

"Ok," I said with a sigh. I needed $15,000 for the down payment and about $20,000 for renovations. This really set me back and crushed my spirits. After leaving the bank, I called Ives to vent, and like always she tried her best to offer solutions. She offered to give me the money I needed for renovations, but I wouldn't accept it. There is no way I am taking $20,000 from her, Grant, or Dean. I would just have to wait until my credit score is back where it needs to be. I calculated all my credit card debt and created a payment plan to get them paid off by the end of the school year. All I need is for my art gallery to be opened before August that gives me about ten months to get it. Every time I think about taking one step forward something happens.

I've stressed myself out enough for the day. Since I knew Dean would be spending another night at the hospital, I thought it would be a good idea to bring him a home-cooked meal. He had been staying there for a week straight. I'm sure he is tired of eating from their cafeteria so, I whipped up some smothered chicken, peas, and rice. On the way to the hospital, I stopped by the florist and bought his mother some flowers. Even though she is still on life support, I wanted her to awake to a beautiful arrangement of flowers. When I arrived at the hospital, I peeked into the room and saw Dean was asleep in the corner. Aunt Bee was sitting at the foot of the bed watching the evening news.

"Hey sweetie," she whispered as she hugged me.

"I brought dinner. I had a feeling you'd be here too, so I made you a plate." I held up the bag as she took it from my hand and went to warm up the containers of food. I walked over to Dean and kissed his cheek. He looked so good in the grey Nike tech sweatsuit he is wearing. He looked so peaceful sleeping with his hat was turned back, and his arms folded over his chest. He was seated on the edge of the chair with his head laid to the side. Before I turned to walk away, he grabbed my thigh.

"What you doing here?" he said with sleep still in his voice. He ran his hand up and down my thigh before gripping it tightly.

"I brought you dinner."

He pulled me into his lap and ran his nose up and down my neck. "Thank you, Chubs." Dean finally opened his eyes and smiled. He adjusted himself in the chair still holding me tightly in his lap.

"Has the doctor given you all any updates?" I asked while looking at Ms. Pam.

He sighed. "Yeah, it's not looking too good. He said we will need to make a 'decision' soon." We sat in silence as I played with his ear until Aunt Bee returned with their food. While they ate, we made small talk with one another. It was evident that they were trying to avoid the fact that Ms. Pam's condition wasn't getting any better. Although Dean seemed to be doing fine I know deep down he is hurting. Aunt Bee lightened the mood by telling me stories about Dean's upbringing.

"This boy has always been a mess," she joked. "But he is still my baby," she said, with a shaky voice. I noticed the tears in her eyes, but she quickly blinked them away and excused herself from the room. I looked at Dean who had tears in his eyes as well.

I grabbed his hand. "Let's go outside." We walked to the elevator hand in hand, while I caressed his hand with my thumb. He gave me a small smile as we walked onto the elevator.

We sat on the bench outside of the hospital. The fall air feels so refreshing. Dean took a deep breath, and his shoulders dropped when he exhaled.

"I'm here for you, babe," I said to him.

He nodded while looking at his hands. "I know, and I appreciate that." When he finally made eye contact with me his eyes held no emotion. I rubbed his back.

"Autumn, I want you to be my woman. No more taking it slow," he said with authority.

The sincere and fervent tone he used let me know this wasn't up for discussion. Dean had been patient with me much longer than expected. He'd showed me how serious he was about us and I feel comfortable giving him my heart. Everything about this go-round felt so right.

I looked at the sky and replied, "Ok."

He grabbed my hand and kissed it. "I love you. You don't have to say it back, but just know I do. I loved you before and after you cut me off. Something about you is different, and you make me different." He leaned over and kissed me before I could respond. Everything he said I felt in our kiss. This moment made me grateful for giving him a second chance.

$\mathcal{D}$ean

AFTER A MONTH, Autumn feels more comfortable about meeting Yaya. Once she revealed to me that she lost a child, everything that happened between us made sense. Truthfully, I'm glad we ended things when we did because it allowed her the time to heal. It was selfish of me to think she was against meeting Yara because she hadn't forgiven me. Not once did I take into consideration that maybe her reservations had nothing to do with me. I will never be able to understand the pain she went through. She suffered something so traumatic while finding out the father of her child was with someone else. Although I wanted nothing more than for them to meet each other, I had to give her time to adjust to our new situation.

Trying to make sure they both had adequate time with me wasn't easy, but Autumn never complained when I would have to cancel plans to be with Yaya. With everything that is going on with my mother, Yaya and Autumn become my escape. Things got heated last time I went to visit my mother at the hospital. The doctor gave an update that I wasn't too happy about. After I cursed my mother's doctor out, Aunt Bee had to intervene. She made me promise not to come back until I got my head right. Every day he entered the room with bad news, and I reached my breaking point. Knowing that I will have to give them permission to let my mother die didn't sit well with me. Between that and overhearing my Aunt discussing funeral arrangements with Uncle Greg, it became too much for me to handle. I haven't been back nor have I talked to Aunt Bee. They couldn't make the final decision without my consent.

Today, Yaya and I are having lunch with Liliana. I was ready to let Lili know I was in a relationship. We met at the deli across the street from the office building where she works. We placed our orders and had small talk while we waited for our food.

"So, how is your mama?" Lili asked.

"Doctor says we may have to make a decision soon." I shook my head. I didn't feel like talking about my mother. That is still a very sore spot for me right now.

She gasped. "Dean, I am so sorry to hear that."

"Yeah." I held my head down. "But I wanted to talk to you about the woman I am involved with. She will be around Yaya, and of course, I want you to be ok with that." I waited for her to finish chewing the food in her mouth.

"I have no problem with that."

"It's complicated, remember the night you popped up at my house and told me you were pregnant? The woman that was with me is who I am dating again."

Lili put her fork back in her salad and took another bite. Before we started working on our friendship and co-parenting, we had an argument about how she ruined my relationship with Autumn. Granted, it was my fault too, but I was hurt and wasn't ready to own up to my part in the situation.

"Oh, I remember her. She probably hates me." We both laughed.

"Nah, she's not like that at all. I just want you and her to get along. She is someone I really care about."

I want to co-parent and have a healthy relationship. Lili and I are cool, but I haven't been in a relationship or anything close to it since Autumn. I wasn't sure how this would turn out.

"I'm cool with her being around Yaya. I hope we can sit down and talk one day. I owe her an apology.

She didn't deserve to be caught in the middle of our mess. Since we are talking about dating..." she took a sip of her water before continuing, "I am back talking to my ex."

The night I met Lili at Linx she told me about how she and her on again, off again boyfriend broke up the day before her birthday. I didn't ask the details behind their break up, but during her pregnancy, I knew they got cool again.

"Ok." I nodded my head. "Are you ready to have him around Yaya?" I looked at Yaya who was enjoying her vegan mac and cheese.

"Yes, I want you to meet him first though. We've been dating for 6 months now. He's actually the friend I went to Miami with a while back."

I like that Liliana and I can sit down and talk about us dating other people without jealousy. This made my life ten times easier. I've heard horror stories about co-parenting gone bad. I have a few friends who have baby mamas from hell.

"Set something up, and I will be there," I said before drinking my water.

"I am so glad we can sit down like two adults and talk about our love lives. It's really refreshing to be able to co-parent the right way," she beamed.

"I agree," I said while letting out a sigh of relief. Autumn will be pleased to hear Liliana is cool with her being around our daughter. Autumn expressed how important it was for her and Liliana to have drama-free interactions with one another. She wasn't the only one who wanted to keep the peace. Now, I can't wait to see her tonight.

"Ahhhhh, Dean," Autumn moaned, as I plunged into her. I came to her house to talk about my lunch with Lili, but I walked in on her in downward facing dog, and it was downhill from there. We didn't even make it out her art studio. I took her down right on her yoga mat. She arched deeper and threw it back creating a steady rhythm for us both. I gripped her waist tighter as she scratched the hardwood floors under us.

"Shit," I grunted.

She turned over and wrapped her legs around my waist. Autumn started moaning louder signaling me that her peak was near.

"Deeper," she whined out. I unwrapped her legs and pushed them to her chest. She grabbed my arms and dug her nails into me. I smiled when her eyes rolled into the back of her head.

"Damn, girl," I said as I felt her warm nectar cover me. She leaned forward and pushed me on my back. After sitting comfortably on me, she started bouncing at a steady pace. I rested my arms behind my head as I watched my baby go to work. She leaned forward taking my bottom lip into her mouth, sucking and licking it while moaning. Grabbing her head, I pulled her closer while I attacked her mouth. We kissed hard and passionately as I reached my peak inside of her. Afterward, she laid on top of me, and I massaged her scalp.

"How was your day?" she asked tiredly.

"It was cool. This made it better," I laughed lightly.

"Me too. I could go for another round," Autumn lifted her head from my chest.

I raised my brow. "Oh, yeah?" I said, gripping her ass before smacking it. She let out a quiet moan and nodded her head. She stood blessing me with the perfect view of her pear shape. I watched hungrily as she sauntered out of the room. Wasting no time I followed behind her to the bedroom. She tried to walk to the bed, but I grabbed her arm and pushed her against the wall. I trailed kisses from her lips down to her perfect breasts. She grabbed my head as I gently sucked on her nipples giving them both equal attention. I continued my trail of kisses down her stomach to her thick thighs. I threw the left leg over my shoulder before I latched onto her now swollen bulb. Her sweet juices covered my lips and tongue as I devoured her. With every suck and lick, she pushed herself closer to me. I ran my right hand over her stomach before using my arm to pin her against the wall.

"Stop running," I hissed, before continuing to eat her like she was my last meal.

"Ah shit," she said before crying out something I couldn't understand. She rocked her hips against my tongue as she reached her peak again. Once she came down, I carried over to the bed and bent her over the edge.

With her legs spread wide, I slowly inched in feeling her wetness cover me. I placed my hand on the middle of her sweaty back making her arch deeper into the bed. She moaned in pleasure as our bodies collided with one another. In no time she reached her peak again and wasn't too far behind.

"I love you," I said in between grunts.

"I love you too," she damn near screamed. No matter how many times she said she loved me, it still made me feel some type of way. After hearing her confess her love for me, I released inside of her again and fell down beside her. She kissed my cheek before falling asleep on my chest. We repeated this routine all weekend.

Before I knew it Monday rolled around and she was leaving for work. The missing piece to my otherwise perfect weekend was Yaya. Typically she would be in daycare, but I called Liliana and told her we were playing hooky today. I missed my baby, we need daddy-daughter time. After picking her up from Liliana's mother's house, we ate breakfast at a vegan-friendly cafe. When she shared her desire for our daughter to be vegan, I was entirely against it. However, after researching and seeing how healthy Liliana eats I was on board. Having to keep fresh food available for Yaya forced me to change my eating habits as well. I do indulge in a nice steak now and then, but mostly, I eat seafood.

After lunch, we went to our favorite place, the park. I try to bring her here at least two times a week she loves the swing and big red slide. Yaya is so charismatic that every time we come she makes a friend. I exchanged numbers with a few parents to keep these random playdates going. Growing up as an only child wasn't as fun as people may think. I spent a lot of time alone, my mother wasn't able to have any children after me. However, I am grateful that she and Aunt Bee made sure Grant, and I had a close relationship. After his sister and my baby cousin, Gabrielle passed away we needed each other. The bond I have with Grant is something I want Yaya and Gabby to share. My hope is to one day give Yaya siblings to grow up with, but I know that won't be for a while since I just got into a relationship. Autumn and I are not ready to have a child together.

Yaya giggled as I gently pushed her on the swing. Whenever she would go forward, she would clap her hands in excitement. The pure happiness my baby shows warms my heart. She has not one care in the world, and I will do all I can to make sure it stays that way. As I pushed her on the swing, we sang the ABC song and I'm noticing Yaya's interest in music. First, the baby piano and now this, music lessons are definitely in her future. The light tap I felt on my shoulder made me grab Yaya's swing.

"Hey stranger," Bre said with a small smile.

I have to find a new park. I thought to myself.

I resumed pushing Yaya before responding, "How you been?" I looked over my shoulder to get a good look at her. Bre had on pink leggings with a matching jacket and her long black hair was pulled into a ponytail. As always she was beautiful, but the feelings I once had for her are gone.

"I've been ok. How about you?" Bre locked arms with me. I pulled my arm out of her hold and laughed.

"I'm ok," I responded disinterestedly. Bre rolled her eyes to try to play off the embarrassment that briefly covered her face. "It was good seeing you," I said while taking Yara out of the swing. She laid her head on my shoulder. Just like that, she was ready for her nap.

"Dean, wait!" Bre ran after me. "I miss you, and I am sorry for the way I acted at the dinner party."

"It's cool. Everything is good," I assured her. Honestly, I haven't thought about her since she stormed out of my club. I guess because soon after Autumn occupied my thoughts and time.

"Let's get drinks and catch up." She stepped closer to me.

Shaking my head, I said, "Can't."

"Wow, it's only been three months, and you've already moved on huh?" Bre folded her arms.

I licked my lip to stop the smile of annoyance that was about to appear. "Sweetheart, we were never serious. Yes, I moved on and you should too." She sucked her teeth and stormed off. I heard her mumble I wasn't shit. I used my hand to muffle the laugh I felt brewing. *That's why I stopped messing with your ass.* Grant was right about how immature younger girls can be. Bre was smart and fun to be around, but her tantrums quickly reminded that she is only 24. The lust I had for her made it easy to ignore them, but now I realize how annoying and unnecessary they were.

After dropping Yaya off at Liliana's mother's house, I drove to Autumn's. Since she left me this morning, she'd been on my mind. I didn't expect to fall for her as hard as I did, but here I am. Last year when I met her at my club, I knew she was different. Autumn's vibe was something I hadn't experienced before. She was easy-going, kind, and selfless. I was used to dating women who wanted to offer nothing but their body. The first night I spent with Autumn, we talked about deep shit, our childhood, dreams, and fears. I was completely caught off guard by the feelings that seemed to have grown overnight. The women I dated after Autumn, left me feeling unfulfilled. Sure I enjoyed the sex, but after experiencing such a deep connection with Autumn, I wanted more. And ever since she's been back in my life that lack of fulfillment has dissipated.

I used my key to enter, the scent of her delicious lasagna welcomed me. When I rounded her kitchen corner, I found her singing along to Sade's *Sweetest Taboo* while swaying her hips from side to side. Quietly and carefully, I crept behind her and wrapped my arms around her waist. I expected her to jump, but she laid her head back against my chest. She continued to make a fresh garden salad as we swayed to the song.

"I didn't scare you?" I whispered against her ear. She shook her head and continued cutting tomatoes as I ran my hands up and down her thighs.

She stopped humming and said, "I smelled your cologne when you walked in the kitchen." She turned to face me and I put my hands on the counter caging her in so she wouldn't move. I used the tip of my tongue to lick her bottom lip before sucking it.

I leaned towards her ear and whispered, "I missed you."

She wrapped her arms around my neck and replied, "I missed you too. Especially after the way you did me this weekend."

"When we finish eating, we can finish where we left off this morning," I said while gripping her butt.

She turned to finish dinner. "What did you do today?"

"I spent time with Yara. I missed her this weekend, but next Saturday we will all be together," I said smiling.

Autumn nodded. "Yup, sure will. How does Liliana feel about all this?"

Her asking about Liliana reminded me we never talked about how lunch was. While she made the finishing touches on dinner, I told her how well the conversation with Liliana went. I assured her Liliana is okay with everything and wants to sit down and talk to her, eventually. Autumn looked relieved to hear everything went smoothly. She released a sigh of relief when I mentioned Lili getting back with her ex.

"Babe, you have nothing to worry about," I said while rubbing her shoulders. "You're it for me, ok?"

Autumn lowered her head in shame, "I know you probably think I'm so insecure, right?"

I shook my head, "No." Grabbing her chin to make her look at me I continued, "I never want you to feel like you have to mask your feelings around me. If you are feeling something tell me so I can adjust what I'm doing." Autumn's eyes lit up as the corners of her mouth formed a smile. "This is all I want to see from you. This beautiful smile."

Autumn

MY RUNNING partner was finally back in shape and ready to go. This morning Ives and I ran our usual three miles together with minimal complaining from her, I was pleasantly surprised but proud. After the first mile and a half, she usually finds a reason to slow down the pace. Not today though, my girl Ivy jogged with a smile on her face. She claimed since it is a new year she wasn't going to be lazy. I'll give her three weeks tops. On our way back to my place I shared with her my plans to meet Yara. I was nervous that she wouldn't be receptive to me. Ivy assured me I would be fine. She has been around Yara since she was born, so I had no choice but to take her word for it. Ivy also pointed out that Dean hadn't brought any other women around her. She said he doesn't play when it comes to his daughter. I smiled at learning how overprotective he is over his baby. After Ivy left, I worked on a painting to help make the time pass by.

My dinner date with Dean and Yara is in an hour, and my nerves were making it hard to find the *perfect* outfit for tonight. Dean said we were going to a vegan restaurant which I found interesting, but I didn't question it. For the first time, painting didn't ease my nerves like I hoped it would. Even with Ivy telling me I had nothing to worry about I was still unsettled.

What if Yara cries as soon as we make eye contact?

What if I'm not stepmother material?

When I entered my twenties, I swore I would never be a *stepmom*. I laughed thinking how quickly things change. On the verge of 31, I am with a man who has a one and a half-year-old.

Dean texted me letting me know he would be here in a few. It's too late to back out now, plus that would only cause a rift in our new relationship. The past month and a half was going smoothly, I can't allow my ridiculous insecurities to mess this up. With only twenty minutes left to get ready, I decided on a pair of dark wash jeans, an oversized sweater, and a pair of knee high boots. I waited too long to do my hair, so I had to settle for a wash-n-go. Moments later, Dean pulled into my driveway. I met him at the door with a bouquet of roses. He made bringing me flowers before dates a habit that I never wanted to stop.

"You ready?" he asked while hugging me.

I nodded before reaching for my coat and purse. When I got into the car, I turned to the back seat and smiled at how beautiful Yara is in person.

"Hi babygirl," I gushed.

She waved and smiled. My heart literally melted. I turned to Dean who was grinning from ear to ear.

"She's beautiful. She looks just like Liliana," I said, as I turned to face forward. Dean reached over and grabbed my hand. During the car ride, we talked about our days. Even Yara chimed in with her gibberish and giggles. *So far so good.*

"Why are we eating at a vegan restaurant?" I asked as Dean looked for parking.

"Yara is a vegan," he stated casually.

"Wow, what made you all decide that?"

"Liliana's idea. She is a vegan and wanted Yara to be vegan as well," he shrugged.

"That's very interesting."

"I was a little against it at first, but it helps me cut back on junk food," he said while turning the car off. "This restaurant isn't fully vegan, but it offers more options than many of our favorites."

The entire dinner I stared at Dean and Yara... entirely transfixed on their interaction with one another.

The way he fed her, tended to her, and the gentle tone he used when speaking to her was all so new to me. Seeing him in full on daddy mode made my heart swell. I was so captivated by them I barely touched any of my food. Trying the vegan tacos Dean recommended was no longer an interest of mine. I was more interested in the beautiful display of fatherhood before me.

"You've barely touched your food, Chubs. Do I need to sit you on my lap and feed you like I do Yaya?" Dean asked while putting a spoon of vegan mac and cheese into Yara's mouth.

I adjusted in my seat before responding, "No, I'm just really mesmerized by you two. Seeing you like this is beautiful. Makes me wonder what type of mother I would've been." I felt my stomach turn at the admittance of thinking about motherhood. I wasn't trying to make it a big deal, so I ate my food. Dean put Yara back in her high chair and grabbed my hand.

"I know you would've and will be a great mom," he said with confidence. I didn't have the heart to tell him that my chances of becoming a mother were slim to none. Instead, I smiled and took a huge gulp from the glass of chardonnay in front of me. The thought of trying to have children again died when my doctor called my cervix incompetent, whatever that means. So, I buried all feelings of being a mother. Adoption or being a step-mom seemed like more viable options. Dean interrupted all the racing thoughts going through my mind by asking what I wanted for dessert. We agreed on a slice of apple pie and non-dairy ice cream. The ride home I was quiet, still consumed by thoughts of motherhood.

After Dean put Yara down for the night, he met me in his bedroom with two wine glasses and a bottle of merlot. I was in the corner sitting on the black suede chaise I love so much. Dean sat the glasses and bottle down on his nightstand before coming and sitting on the end of the chaise.

"What's on your mind?" he asked, searching my eyes for an answer.

I sat up before responding, "What if I can't get pregnant again?" Asking that dreadful question aloud made tears brew.

Dean grabbed my arms pulling me into his lap. "Babe, don't think like that. Women have miscarriages and go on to have a healthy pregnancy." He kissed my ear then hugged me tightly.

"I know, but still," I mumbled. "What if we decide we want children and I can't?"

Dean sat quietly thinking over a question I'd been asking myself since we got back together. He rubbed his hands down my arms and said, "We will cross that bridge when we get there. Just know that's not a deal breaker for me. There are plenty of options if we have a hard time conceiving, ok?" he grabbed my chin making me look at him. "When you become my wife, Yaya will be just as much your family as she is mine. So don't think you have to have a child to make our family complete. As far as I'm concerned having you and Yaya already completes my idea of the perfect family." I sat speechless in his lap, and he continued to hug and kiss me. I released from his embrace and went to pour our glasses of wine. After taking a sip, I walked back over to Dean and sat beside him.

"Thank you for being so considerate of my past, waiting to meet Yara, and making me feel better about my insecurities. You're making it easy to fall for you more each day." I knew deep down Dean had a soft side and a sympathetic and compassionate heart. He does all he can to hide it, but when he's around Yara and me, it shows so effortlessly. We cuddled up on the chaise, found a movie for us to watch, and eventually fall asleep to.

———

Waking up in Dean's arms is a feeling that's indescribable. No matter how many nights we did this, I always woke up feeling happy and content. Today was no different I woke up on cloud nine, the conversation Dean and I had last night had me at peace. Having Dean confirm that he would be with me even if we have a hard time conceiving calmed the anxiety I didn't realize I had. That was the exact definition of unconditional love. Something I never had, and now I don't want to live without. After relishing in being in his embrace, I removed his arms from around me to get out of bed.

"Where are you going?" he reached for my arm.

"I'll be back." I giggled as he pulled me back into bed.

"Nah, I need you here." he nuzzled his face in my neck. "You know what today is?" he whispered in my ear.

"It's Saturday?" I said confused. I racked my brain for what he meant.

"Yeah, so you know we are going to brunch. Then whatever else you want," he kissed my temple. I blushed, he remembers our tradition.

"Ok, I'll go shower and get ready. Yara coming too?" I asked.

"If you don't mind."

"Not at all." I smiled.

While Dean got dressed, I took out some paint I had in my duffle bag and an 8 x 10 canvas. Yara crawled over to where I was sitting in the middle of his living room floor. I grabbed a paper plate from the kitchen cabinet and poured enough paint for her to use her fingers to paint. I dipped her index and middle fingers into the paint. Yara stared at her fingers unsure of what to do next. I dipped my index and middle finger into the paint then pressed them onto the canvas. Her eyes followed my movements. Like a light bulb went off in her head, she pushed her paint covered fingers onto the canvas. We both covered the canvas with our fingers. Yara became a little too excited sticking her entire hand into the yellow paint and planting it onto the center of the painting. She looked at me for confirmation that her actions were ok.

I smiled and said, "Good job, Yara." Her infectious smile appeared making me smile harder. We planted our hands on the canvas until it was completely covered with paint.

Dean walked behind us and scared us both when he asked, "Can I have this?"

I turned around with Yara in my arms and replied, "Of course." He leaned down to kiss us on the forehead before sitting on the couch in front of us.

"Yaya usually isn't a fan of having her hands dirty." He looked at us and smiled. The twinkle in his eyes made my heart skip a beat.

"Da-da look," Yara said, as she pointed to the canvas in front of us.

"I see baby. You and Autumn did that?" He asked while picking up the canvas and taking a closer look. She nodded her head and giggled. Dean took Yara from my lap so I could wash my hands and clean up our mess. He cleaned up Yara and changed her shirt we accidentally got paint on.

After brunch, we went to a special exhibit that was

only in town for a few more days. I was a little concerned the sculptures would bore that Yara. She proved me wrong pointing at every piece saying "look" in amazement. Yara warmed up to me after our paint session, the entire time we walked around the exhibit, she was in my arms. She even turned from Dean when he tried to take her. I think he was a little salty at first, but then I caught him staring at the both of us with the same twinkle from this morning. We caught the end of a light show before leaving to take Yara to an indoor play center. Dean said it's the quickest way to get her ready for nap time, so we played there for an hour before heading home. Not only was Yara ready for a nap, so was I. While Dean put Yara down, I started on my lesson plans for the upcoming school week. Dean went into his office to answer a call, that felt strange to me. Instead of questioning him I listened to the call outside the door.

"Aunt Bee, I'm not ready to make that decision yet," he whispered. He went silent as he listened to Aunt Bee. He sighed, "I know, I know. I'm just not ready yet. I-" He stopped talking again. "What?" he raised his voice. "Come on, Aunt Bee!" I heard the wheels of his office chair rolling across his hardwood floors, so stepped away from the door and went back into his bedroom. After he ended the call with his aunt, he came back into the room. I could tell the phone call wasn't pleasant. Dean stepped into the room with his fists and jaw clenched tight. His nostrils flared as he inhaled and exhaled forcefully.

"Everything ok?" I asked, giving him the opportunity to tell me the truth. Closing my planner and placing it on top of my bag I walked over to him. He looked down at me and shook his head.

"Everyone is ready to give up on my mom," his voice shaking. "But I'm not." I wrapped my arms around his neck and pulled his head to my shoulder. He relaxed in my arms as I rubbed the back of his neck.

"Babe, no one is giving up on her," I whispered into his ear.

"I've heard of people who stay on life support for years and recover."

"Me too, but unfortunately I don't think your mother will be one of those cases. She is completely brain dead. Her organs are slowly shutting down as well. The machine is only prolonging the inevitable," I said as sympathetically as possible. He pulled back and looked me in the eyes. His eyes narrowed as he removed his arms from my waist.

"I think you should go," he said leaving out of his room.

I followed behind him. Grabbing his shoulder, I asked, "Why?"

"I'm not in the best mood right now, and I don't want to take it out on you," he snarled. He peeked into Yaya's room before walking down the steps.

Still, on his heels, I responded, "So, that's it? Whenever you're in a bad mood or I say something you don't like I have to leave?" I folded my arms over my chest.

"Autumn, you nor anyone else understands what I'm going through," he hissed. Dean walked towards me until I was against the wall. "I am being forced to make a decision I'm not comfortable with. Do you know how it feels to watch my mother lay unconscious knowing she won't wake up? The moment the doctor told us the severity of her injuries, I knew what I had to do, but I kept the hope that she would pull through. My mother is my lifeline. Before you and Yara it was her." he blew out a harsh breath. I watched his shoulder slump as he walked away from me. Dean has already started the grieving process. Him thinking she would pull through was denial, now anger.

"If anyone understands what you're going through it's me," I yelled before looking upstairs, knowing we could wake Yara, I lowered my voice, "Dean, I'm on your side, but it isn't fair to Ms. Pam, Aunt Bee or you to keep prolonging this. I see the pain in your eyes every time we go to the hospital." I reached for his arm just to have him pull away from me. He shook his head before heading back upstairs to his office

Not wanting to cause an argument, I packed my things so he could take me home. The car ride was intense, Dean gripped the steering wheel tighter and tighter until his hands were red. Yara was still sleeping peacefully in her car seat. I didn't waste my words by saying anything before exiting the car. I kissed his cheek and blew a kiss at Yaya before getting out.

After a few hours passed, I called Dean to see if he'd calm down. Three phone calls later, still no answer. I'm assuming he didn't answer because he is busy working, so I text him. I figured when he freed up he would respond.

Autumn: Just checking in. I'm here when you're ready to talk.

I expected hours to go by before he texted me back, but as soon as I pressed send his response came through.

Dean: Thanks, I appreciate that.

The grey bubble appeared, and I waited for him to say more, but he never did. Several hours later he still hadn't responded. I don't know how we will make it if he keeps distancing himself from me.

IT'S BEEN two days since I heard from Dean. He hasn't been answering my calls or texts. I decided to pop up at his house to see what was going on with him. There was a part of me hoping he wasn't out cheating on me, but I knew better than that. Dean fully opened his heart to me he wouldn't jeopardize what we had like that. When I pulled into his driveway, I noticed his car wasn't there it must be in the garage. It's Monday night, so I knew he would be resting from the busy weekend he had at his clubs. I opened his front door, and the entire downstairs was pitch black. I heard a noise coming from his room I slowly walked up the stairs bracing myself for whatever I was about to step into. After pushing the door open, I saw him sitting at the edge of his bed with his head in his hands. I ran over to him and got on my knees to remove his hands.

"Babe, what's wrong?" I asked as I wiped tears from his face. Dean pulled his hands away from me and stood up.

"What are you doing here, Autumn?" he walked over to his closet and put on a t-shirt. Whenever he called me by my name, I knew shit was about to hit the fan. He was very consistent with the nicknames he gives people.

"I haven't heard from you in days," I charged over to the closet. I didn't appreciate the way he was speaking to me. His tone was so cold and dissociated. This isn't the Dean I knew. The Dean I am head over heels in love with.

"Needed some space," he tried to brush past me, but I held my arms up blocking him. His nostrils flared as he took in a deep breath. "Autumn, move."

"No! Why have you been distant? Is it something I did? Talk to me." I put my hand on his chest, and he took a step back. I didn't know the fight we had the other day would lead to this. The look in his eyes held no emotion, no warmth.

"Baby, talk to me," I pleaded with him. While caressing his cheek I waited for him to open up. He looked down at me and shook his head. He removed my hand and moved me to the side as he left the closet.

"I just need to be alone right now," he said with his back towards me. Tears started to fill my eyes. It bothered me that he could shut me out so quickly, but I couldn't force him to be open with me.

"Dean?" I called his name unsure about what I'm feeling.

"I need some time, Autumn." He continued to get dressed as I stood like a statue in the middle of his closet. After wiping away the tears that had fallen, I left his closet to go home. When I finally reached home, I crawled into bed and cried some more. I felt like this was the beginning of the end for us.

One. Whole. Week. That's how long it been since I last heard from Dean. I have been losing my mind waiting for him to come back to his senses and realize how fucked up he was acting. The cold February weather made me feel even worse. It had been snowing for a few hours now, and all I could think about was being snuggled under Dean as we listened to music. However, I knew that wasn't happening so instead I turned on my music and let my brush flow freely on the canvas in front of me. All I wanted was for him to pick up the phone and let me know he was ok. It hurt me that he could go this long without any contact with me. If anyone understands what he's going through, it's me.

Show Me by Amerie played, and I thought about how the words expressed precisely how I feel about Dean. When I saw him at Grant's dinner, I knew I wanted him back, but I had to protect my heart. Guarding my heart went out the window the day he told me he loved me, every wall I tried to keep up came crumbling down. Now, I'm lovesick, and I miss him. I miss us.

A call interrupted the song playing, I looked at the caller ID and saw Dean's name.

"Hey," I whispered, unsure of how this conversation could go.

"You home?" he asked.

I put my paintbrush and palette down before responding, "Yes."

"I'm outside," he said before hanging up.

After washing my hands, I rushed downstairs to let him in. A part of me wondered why he didn't just use his key, but that wasn't important. I am happy he is here. I opened the door to him in a grey hoodie covered by denim jacket, grey joggers, and his infamous red Nike dad hat. Even with it snowing he was dressed like it's early fall. Not sure if we should hug or not, I stepped to the side so he could come in.

Once I closed the door and took a deep breath,

"Please let this conversation go well," I said a short prayer before meeting him in the living room.

He stood in the middle of my living room with his hands in his pockets contemplating what to say or do. As happy as I am that he is here I couldn't get too comfortable. A whole week without hearing from him is unacceptable, and he needed to know. When we decided we were going to be together, we promised to be open about everything. Dean makes me feel more than I've ever felt with any other man. He has changed me in ways I can't begin to explain. However, I will never be anyone's fool ever again. No matter how much I love him.

We spoke at the same time.

"Babe.."

"Look.."

"You go first," I said as I took a seat on my couch. Last time I saw Dean, he didn't have much to say.

"I've been doing a lot of thinking the past few days." He took a seat next to me. "My mom is my world. I don't know what I am going to do without her. It's hard to process, and it's hard to sit by and watch her die. On top of that, I have to be a father to Yaya and this relationship.."

I knew where this was going, but I didn't want to believe that he would do this to me.

I cut him off, "What are you saying?"

He turned to me, there was a hint of sadness in his

eyes as he spoke, "I'm saying we need to take a break until I can fully process everything that is happening around me." In a matter of seconds, I went from frustrated to sad to enraged back to calm. There was nothing I could say or do. He made up his mind.

"That's it?" My voice began to crack, "You end us just like that?" I snapped my fingers.

"I'm not ending us I just need some time," he said avoiding eye contact with me.

"Some time?" I choked out. On the verge of tears, I hurried to the door to escort Dean out. He turned to speak, but before he could I shut the door in his face. With my back against the door, I slid down as tears fell. After my cries settled, I called Grant to set up a time for him and me to meet and talk. If anyone knows how to deal with Dean, it's him. Dean said he needed space, but I would not give up on us that easy. Grant suggested we meet at the hospital which was perfect because we needed input from Aunt Bee as well. I greeted Aunt Bee, Grant, and Ives before the three of us stepped out to have a much-needed conversation.

"I overheard the conversation you had with Dean last week," I said to Aunt Bee. "It turned into us having an argument and him asking me to leave. He thinks we are all giving up on Ms. Pam. I tried my best to explain that's not the case, but we all know how he can be. Today he came by and said he needed space. Our relationship was doing great, and now he's pushing me away."

Grant and Aunt Bee both nodded before Grant spoke, "Dean has a hard time handling things that are out of his control." He explained Dean's behaviors during his parent's divorce. It surprised me to hear they didn't speak for almost a year.

Aunt Bee chimed in, "Dean and his father having an estranged relationship makes this even harder. He feels like he has no parents after we lay my sister to rest." We stood in silence everyone consumed with their own thoughts on the situation.

"I will talk to him," Grant said with finality. I looked to Aunt Bee for confirmation, and she nodded. "He listens to me, so we just need to sit down and chop it up about what he's feeling before it gets worse."

11

*D*ean

"WHAT DID I tell you not to do to Autumn?" Grant asked as we sat at my bar. He called me to meet up to watch the game. I didn't expect him to bring up Autumn though.

I took a sip of my drink before responding, "G, go somewhere with all that." I haven't talked to Autumn since I told her I needed space. She texted me a few times asking to talk. The only problem is I didn't feel like talking to her or anyone. No matter how many times I said how I felt about taking my mom off life support no one listened. When Grant called, I expected him to lecture me, but instead, he mentioned watching the game. I should've known he had ulterior motives because I've been avoiding Aunt Bee and Autumn.

I didn't expect our relationship to turn like this after the great weekend we had. Seeing Autumn and Yaya painting together gave me a glimpse into how our life would be together. The way Yaya became comfortable with Autumn and allowing her to hold her most of the day made my heart full. I knew introducing them was a big step and it would take our relationship to a new level. Sadly, I single-handedly messed that up. When Aunt Bee called me giving me an ultimatum it brought the sadness I was trying to mask front and center. I had no idea my mother made Aunt Bee and myself her power of attorney. Aunt Bee was quick to let me know she would make the final decision without me. Autumn was trying her best to make me feel better. Since she was the only one around, I inadvertently took my anger out on her which she didn't deserve. I asked her to leave so I wouldn't continue to use her as a verbal punching bag. I took a week to think about what I was doing wrong. So I figured we could take a break until I was able to accept that I have to let my mother go. Autumn took me wanting a break the wrong way, and I'm guessing she went to Grant to get advice.

"Bro, I told you not to push her away," he said interrupting my thoughts.

Shaking my head, I said, "That wasn't my intention." I took another sip of my drink and turned my attention to the game. We sat in silence watching the game until it reached half-time, then I felt Grant staring. I downed the last of my drink before turning to him. "Just say it."

"You are going to mess this up if you don't get your shit together," he scolded.

I nodded before signaling the bartender to give me another drink. "After talking to Aunt Bee last week, my thoughts were all over the place. I know that I have to give the doctor the go on pulling the plug. I know my mother isn't ever going to wake up. I know all of that. So Aunt Bee, Autumn, and you constantly reminding me of that does nothing, but make me even more guilty for prolonging this." The bartender slid my drink to me, and I took another sip. "I wasn't trying to hurt Autumn. I just needed time to myself."

"Have you talked to her? Did you think maybe she's concerned about you? She lost her mother a few years ago. I'm sure that pain is still fresh. Yet she's by your side making sure you're good." Grant shook his head. "You was trying to get right with her for over a year. Now that you have her don't mess this up. You might not get another chance...a break?" He chuckled. "You better hope she doesn't go running back to ole boy."

I clenched my jaw. Grant knew just what to say to piss me off. "Ok, I get it." I finished the rest of my drink then slammed my glass down. "I'm doing what I think is best for us. For her. I love Autumn with every fiber of my being, but I'm not in a good mental or emotional place right now. I can't give her my all right now."

Grant nodded, "Just let her be there for you that's all she's trying to do. She understands what you're going through. You're over thinking. Stop putting these crazy expectations on yourself and let her love you. Call her." He stood to put on his coat.

"The game isn't over yet," I said watching him prepare to leave.

"I have a wife and baby to get home to. I'm not trying to end up in the doghouse," he chuckled. "Oh, and you need to call my mom back before she comes to you." He gave me a look that showed how serious Aunt Bee was on her threat. Last time I talked to Aunt Bee, she told me I had a week to get my mind together, or I would have hell to pay. Shaking my head, I went to my office to call her and solidify the meeting with my mother's doctor.

STANDING at the foot of my mother's bed I watched as the doctor's removed all IV's and tubes from my mother. The nurse slowly turned off the ventilator that had been supplying her with oxygen. The only people allowed in the room are myself and Aunt Bee. She held my hand tightly as we watched the doctor and nurses work. Afterward, my aunt said a prayer for us and the doctor said his condolences. I kissed my mother's forehead one final time before leaving her room. When we walked to the waiting room where we were met by Grant, Uncle Greg, Ivy, baby Gabs, Liliana, Yaya, and surprisingly Autumn. Everyone stood and rushed over to us. Autumn hugged me tightly. I didn't realize how much I needed Autumn's embrace until I let my weight fall onto her.

She whispered, "I'm here for you." I nodded because I believed her. Even after I told her I needed space, she made sure to be here for me. I had no expectations of her showing up today, but seeing her meant so much to me. When we released from our embrace, Liliana walked over and handed Yaya to me. I hugged my baby so tight while showering her with kisses. Tears were starting to fill my eyes so, I excused myself from the room. I didn't notice someone was following behind me until Autumn grabbed my hand to stop me. She cupped my cheek before kissing me softly on the lips. I searched her eyes for any sign of anger or hurt, but all I saw was sympathy for me. When I opened my mouth to speak, she pressed her index finger against my lip and shook her head.

"Not today," she said so calmly it made my racing heart slow down.

She removed her finger, and I rushed to speak, "Thank you for being here, Chubs. I need another one of your hugs." I smiled for the first time today. She smiled back as she wrapped her arms around my neck. While we were alone and she was in my arms, I couldn't let another moment go by without letting her know how I felt. "I'm so sorry for trying to push you away," I whispered. She rubbed my back and continued to hug me. "I love you, and I don't want this to be the end for us."

"Dean, I know you were trying your best to make sense of your mother passing," she said with affection in her voice. "I am here because I love you and I know this is a tough time for you. We will talk about us later." I nodded before giving her a quick peck. We shared another hug before going back to check on everyone. Grant came over and hugged me tighter than he'd ever done before.

"Remember, we are all here for you." He turned and looked around the room. I looked at everyone from Aunt Bee to Autumn to Ivy. Everyone in the room was showing signs of sadness. My mother touched everyone in this room. Selfishly, I thought I was the one suffering the most. But after taking a good look at everyone, I saw I wasn't the only who lost someone important today. Grant patted me on the back before returning to his wife and baby. Everyone shared their goodbyes and coordinated a time to meet tomorrow for breakfast. Autumn grabbed my hand as we walked to my car.

"Let's go home," Autumn said as she opened the passenger door.

LAST NIGHT the doctors took my mother off life support, and I have been numb since. My phone has been ringing off the hook. Calls from family members I haven't seen since childhood, my mother's old coworkers, and people I don't even know flooded my voicemail. After the sixth call from G, I turned my phone off. For three months, I have been praying she would wake from her coma. I prayed fervently this is all a dream that I would wake up from. Sitting in her living room crying as I looked at pictures of us is not where I thought I'd be.

Walking through the empty rooms that were once filled with love and joy had my heart breaking. I sat on my mother's bed and looked at every detail of her room. She had a basket of laundry on the floor that she never got to fold. My mother hated leaving clean towels unfolded because it causes wrinkles, so I emptied the basket on the bed and began folding. I opened her closet in her bedroom and turned on the light. She told me if anything ever happened to her to go in the safe, but not a moment before. I always laughed her off thinking she'd be here forever. But my mother being someone who was prepared made sure to leave me something. After punching in the code, my birthday, I sorted through the boxes she had stacked in the back. There were three boxes, one labeled Yara, Dean, and future grandbaby. Slowly I opened the boxes, my mouth fell open at the contents inside. There were stacks upon stacks of money. At the bottom of the box addressed to me, there was a letter telling me to add the money to the trust funds for my children and how much she loves me. I closed all of the boxes and did a final sweep of the safe and found a box with diamond earrings that I placed in my pocket.

Before leaving her room, I took the quilt she made off her bed to give to Yara. She's too young to remember her grandmother this quilt will be something she can keep forever and pass down to her children. Knowing she won't be here for my wedding, Yara's first day of school or the birth of future grandchildren causes a pang of sadness to come over me. Afterward, I looked at all the pictures she had hanging on the walls in the hallway. I took down the pictures she had of Grant, Gabrielle, and I when we went to Disney world as kids. I ran my fingers across the image of my dad holding me on my first night home from the hospital, and finally the picture of me kissing her as she held my degree. I came here to get pictures for my Aunt Bee to use in her funeral program. Thankfully, my aunt took over because I couldn't stomach planning my mother's funeral.

"This is harder than I ever imagined," I said to myself. As I was leaving out the front door, I noticed a car parked out front.

"I know this isn't who I think it is," I gritted my teeth. The timing of me seeing my father couldn't be more off. He was the absolute last person I wanted to see. His presence would do nothing but piss me off more.

"Son, we need to talk," he said as I walked to my car.

"I don't have shit to say to you," I spat while opening my car door.

"Well then, listen to what I have to say." He reached for my shoulder.

I stepped back. "Don't touch me."

"I was with your mother for almost 30 years before we divorced! Don't you think it bothers me that someone shot her after she left from a meeting with me?"

"What? No one ever told me that." My heart raced as I looked at the ground. The police report did mention my mother hugging someone before leaving the restaurant. Why were they at dinner together? My father read the questioning look on my face, so he went on to the explain the events leading up to my mother being robbed and shot.

"I came to the hospital to tell you, but you walked out. The night your mother was robbed she was leaving from having dinner with me. We met to talk about you. For months I have been trying to reach out to you to no avail. The last time we met, she showed me pictures of you and our grandbaby. Son, I'm sorry. I just wanted another chance to fix our family," he said sincerely.

Anger consumed my body, this is all my fault. Had I not been so stubborn and called like she asked she would still be here. My father hugged me as I sobbed in his arms. All this hate and resentment I am harboring cost me my mother's life. Everything around me went quiet as I stood there stuck. I fell back onto my car and ran my hands down my face.

"I have to go," I said while staring straight ahead. My father nodded before walking back to his car. I didn't know how to feel after finding out the events that led to my mother's death. After starting my car, I drove to Grant's house ready to share with everyone what my father shared with me.

THE SPRING AIR sent a chill through my body as the preacher said the Lord's prayer before lowering my mother's casket into the ground. This is the day I never wanted to happen, Autumn held my hand tightly while Grant held my shoulder. Tears ran down my eyes as I watched her black and gold casket get lowered into the ground. I threw the red rose I had been holding on to for dear life down with her. Flashbacks of every special moment we shared played through my mind as the casket got lower and lower. On March 1, 2018, a piece of me died along with my mother. I said my final goodbyes before walking back to the black Escalade truck that is taking the family to the repast.

While taking hugs and condolences from the family and friends, I saw my father off to the side looking just as hurt as I feel. During dinner, Aunt Bee and Uncle Greg sat with him to keep him company. I wasn't sure what to say or do, but eventually, I worked up the nerve to go talk to him. When he saw me walking over the sadness in his eyes was replaced with hope. Without thinking, I hugged him tight he returned the hug.

"I'm so sorry, son," he kept repeating that over and over while rubbing my back.

"It's not your fault." I released from our hug. "I'm sorry for taking so long to forgive you. It should've never come to this." I shook my head. "We need to get our relationship back on track sooner than later."

"I agree, son."

My father and I shared another long hug before he left. If my mother dying has taught me anything it's that life cannot be taken for granted and forgiveness is necessary not for my father, but for me. My father was doing all he could to rectify his mistakes. No one is perfect, and we all make mistakes. Myself included, I tried to push my woman away, that almost cost me the love of my life. I am grateful Autumn could forgive me for my moment of selfishness and stand by me during this tough time. When my father and I ended our conversation, Autumn walked behind me and grabbed my hand. With our fingers intertwined I brought her hand to my lips.

"I'm proud of you," she said as she laid her head on my shoulder.

"My mother has been asking me to talk to him for months. I have to do what's right. It's what she wanted." I sighed. If I knew then what I know now, I would've called the first time she brought him up. I looked back at my father who was getting in his car. "And he is the only parent I have left." Aunt Bee came over with a smile on her face. The first time I'd seen her smile in two weeks.

"Baby, I am so proud of you for wanting to work things out with your father. Pam would be so proud," she grabbed my cheeks.

———

TWO MONTHS LATER...

"This is for you, Ma," I said after kissing the angel chain I bought in her memory. After many conversations over the phone, my father and I are finally meeting up for lunch. I can't lie I am nervous as hell. I'm not sure what I am going to say once we are face to face. Over the phone, we apologized to each other, reminisced about the good times, and made small talk. Talking to him a few times a week filled the void of talking to my mother.

My father walked into the restaurant, and I waved my hand to get his attention. When our eyes met one another his face lit up. Then I realized how much my father and Yara have the same smile.

"Son, it's good to see you again," he said, happiness in his voice.

"Good to see you too, Pops," I replied just as happy.

Once we were settled, I pulled out my phone and showed him pictures of my babygirl. I would've brought her today, but Liliana took her to visit their family in Florida for the week. The smile on my father's face as he scrolled through videos and pictures of Yaya was priceless. He stopped on the image of her and Autumn from our day at the museum.

"Who is this beautiful woman?" he asked with his left brow raised.

I couldn't help the smile that appeared, "That's my woman, Autumn."

He nodded in approval, "Lucky man. It looks Yara has taken a liking to her."

"She has," I said confirming his observation. "Watching them interact gives me a glimpse into what our family dynamic will be like when we get married."

My father leaned back as his eyes widened. "Marriage? I haven't heard you say that word in a while."

I chuckled, "Yeah, Pops. She's definitely the one. I almost messed it up, but she has such a big heart, she forgave me. She has taught me a lot about love and myself."

My father became unusually quiet as he tapped his fingers on the table sorting through his thoughts. The years of not talking to or seeing him made me forget how much I look like him. His dark brown skin shows no signs of aging. His beard has more gray hairs than the last time I saw him. My father's deep-set eyes showed a hint of sadness before he spoke, "Son, I want you to know my past indiscretions had nothing to do with you or your mother. It was all me. I was selfish, and again I'm just so sorry for hurting you. For breaking our family apart."

"Pops, it's all good. I forgive you." And I meant that. The animosity I was harboring toward him only caused me more hurt in the long run. The duration of our lunch we talked about my clubs and his life in retirement. I know we still have a while before we are 100 percent good, but I feel we are on track to being close again.

Like Autumn and I, after the funeral, I had a lot of making to do for the way I treated her It took a while before we were good again. For a while, we were just ok. I know relationships have their ups and downs, but the downs we had, man. I shook my head thinking about the nights we spent apart. Even though she was by my side every step of the way and said, she forgave me. I still felt guilty. Every day I have been making up for it by working to buy that space she wanted for her art studio. Ivy informed me that Autumn wasn't approved for enough money to cover the down payment and renovations. I met with the real estate broker as well as contractors to make my baby's dream come to life. Ivy, Grant, and I were working quickly and quietly to have this space ready in time.

Every time I brought up the art studio to Autumn, her mood would change. She never went into detail about why she stopped looking into spaces. There was always a new excuse she made up, but funding was never one of them. Ivy mentioned how Autumn is too prideful to accept money from us. Since I knew the real reason behind her backing out of following through on her dream, I wouldn't start an argument.

After my lunch with my father, Ivy and I signed the contract for Autumn's gallery. I planned on giving it to her as a birthday gift. On the ride over to her future gallery, I couldn't stop the happiness that overcame me. Her birthday is two weeks from now, I would have to keep this under wraps a little longer.

Originally I planned a trip for us to go to Hawaii for the week. But Autumn hadn't been feeling well lately, so I had to come up with a better plan. While I headed across town to meet the contractors Grant put me in contact with, Ivy went to check on my Chubs. I figured it was just a stomach bug she'd gotten from one of her students. Last week Autumn mentioned one of them having the stomach flu. Ever since then my baby has been throwing up every meal she ate. Thinking about how sick she's been made me want to rush home to her, but what I'm doing for her is guaranteed to make her feel better about everything.

12

*A*utumn

I WIPED AWAY the sweat beads from my forehead before releasing the remnants of my breakfast into the toilet bowl. Since Monday night, this is where I have spent most of my time. Ivy told me if I didn't feel better by day three she was coming over with her mom's soup. Which I had no problem with since my appetite has increased immensely. Yet I couldn't hold any of my meals down. Last week, I had two students who had the stomach flu, I'm starting to think they passed their sickness to me. I flushed the toilet before washing cold water over my face.

What is wrong with you, girl? I asked my reflection.

Slowly, I dragged myself back to my grey, suede sectional sofa and resumed binging *Dear White People*. My doorbell woke me from my impromptu nap. After checking the time I realized who the visitors were. Ivy quickly maneuvered herself with a baby bag, a bag of food, and car seat to my living room. She unstrapped Gabby and removed her denim jacket. I sat on the edge of my sofa, waiting for her to fire off questions.

"How are you feeling?" she whispered, Gabby was asleep, and I assumed Ivy wanted to keep it that way.

"Tired," is all I could muster up. Ivy nodded before disappearing into my kitchen with her bags of food. I watched my Godbaby sleep peacefully in her car seat, her cheeks had gotten so fat over the last few months. She definitely had Grant's face, there was no denying that. After several minutes, Ives returned with a tray of soup and cornbread and a cup of water.

"This should make you feel a little better." She placed the tray over my lap.

I wasted no time digging into the food before me. Ives observed as I scarfed down her mother's soup and cornbread. The expression on her face showed there was something on her mind. I pray it isn't what I think it is.

"You know, during my second trimester I had an appetite like that," Ivy said wide-eyed.

Stopping mid-chew, I asked, "What are you trying to say?"

"Last time you were pregnant did you get this sick?"

I took a sip of my water. "Ives, stop. I'm not pregnant. I caught a stomach bug from my students." *I can't be pregnant,* I thought as tears formed. Pregnancy was the first thing I thought about when I began feeling sick, but I pushed it to the back of my mind. After my miscarriage, I had convinced myself that I was unable to conceive another child.

"It's ok." Ives grabbed my hand and squeezed it.

Shaking my head fervently I said, "No, it's not." The fear of losing another baby caused my heart to beat rapidly.

"Autumn, it's going to be ok," Ivy said while hugging me. "When was your last period?"

I shrugged, "I don't know." Reaching for my phone, I opened my period tracker app and scrolled through the last few months. "I've been stressed with not being able to open my gallery, and my relationship with Dean was on the rocks for a minute." I quickly listed possible reasons why I'm late trying to convince myself more than her.

Ives gave me a side eye. "Let me see your phone." Her eyes widened at the revelation of my last cycle. "February? It's May, sis. You've never been this late before." She handed my phone back to me.

The thought of possibly being pregnant made me nauseous. Running to the bathroom, I emptied my stomach of the few spoonfuls of soup I ate. Ivy waited by the door as I washed my mouth out with water. She folded her arms over her chest on my way back to the sofa I avoided eye contact with her.

"I'll make an appointment with my doctor," I said before drinking my water. She stood in front of me with her arms still folded. "And I will tell Dean when he comes over tonight." I rolled my eyes. Although, I much rather wait until I visit my doctor. There's no sense in getting him excited if it wasn't true. While staring at my period tracker hoping to find an inaccuracy, I received a text from my student, Rayna.

Rayna: Hi Ms. Richardson, I know you said only text you when it's an emergency. But you haven't been here all week, and I wanted to share with you that... I GOT ACCEPTED INTO NYU!!!!

"Yes!" I yelled aloud before responding

Ms. Richardson: Congratulations! I knew you would get in! When I return to work, I will have a special gift for you! Xoxo.

I knew Rayna would be accepted into the program. She is way too talented for them to deny her. Although I am extremely proud of Rayna, it's bittersweet because she would be the last baby I helped get into an art program before ending my teaching career. Remembering that in a few months I would be let go from my job made my stomach turn. I'm still trying to figure out a plan b since my art gallery won't be happening anytime soon. I touched my stomach and took a deep breath; if there is a bundle of love in here, I need to quickly find a means of income.

My stomach finally settled, and I was able to hold down a meal. I thanked Ivy for coming to check on me and snuggled on the couch preparing for a nap.

When I opened my eyes, I saw Dean standing over me with his hand on my forehead. I smiled at the look of concern that covered his face while he felt for a fever. He leaned down to kiss my forehead before walking into the kitchen. I heard water running and cabinets closing. Shortly after, my teapot started to whistle letting Dean know the water he put on reached boiling temperature. A few moments later he returned with a cup of tea.

"My mother used to make ginger tea with honey when I was sick as a kid." He placed the cup of tea down on the coffee table. "How are you feeling, baby?"

I sat up and replied, "I'm ok. I was able to eat some soup today." He handed me the tea to drink. Dean observed as I sipped the tea. This wasn't regular ginger tea. I tasted the hint of cinnamon and nutmeg he added. I moaned at how delicious this cup of tea tastes. He smiled and kissed my temple before standing. "Where are you going?" I grabbed his arm.

"I'm going to change out of these clothes. I'll be right back." He gave me a reassuring smile. Our relationship had been a little off, one week we were great... the next, just ok.

We both were trying our best to get out of this funk

we were in. It was clear we wanted to be together, but unsure of how to get back on track. Dean was doing his best to grieve the death of his mother and continue his everyday routine. I commend him for the way he kept his head high during this tough time. After we laid Ms. Pam to rest, Dean apologized for his behavior the weeks before. At first, I was hurt, I felt like he was giving up on us, but I had to put myself in his shoes. He doesn't know how to let people be there from him. The conversation I had with Grant and Aunt Bee put a lot in perspective for me. It was easy for me to forgive him because I knew he sincerely didn't mean to hurt me.

After he returned from changing his clothes, he laid behind me on the sofa. He wrapped his arms around me and held me close. "I love you so much, Chubs." His warm breath against my ear sent chills down my spine.

"I love you too," I said smiling. I turned to face him, "I don't think I have the stomach flu." Dean's brows wrinkled as he adjusted himself. "My period is late." My eyes widened as I waited for his reaction.

"How late?" he asked calmly.

"A few months," I whispered, before biting the inside of my jaw. A glimmer of excitement flickered in his eyes. He sat up on the sofa. "I have an appointment tomorrow morning," I shrugged.

"Ok," he nodded. There was an awkward silence, my heart rate increased with every passing moment.

"You don't have anything to say?" I asked nervously.

He grabbed my face and said, "No, I'm aware of what you went through your last pregnancy. If we are pregnant, we will take it a day at a time."

I nodded as tears formed in my eyes. Dean tenderly kissed my cheeks and wiped away a tear that had fallen. "Everything is going to be ok." I don't know if he was trying to play it cool because I was visibly nervous or if he was really ok with the possibility of me being pregnant. Either way, I am grateful for Dean and his support.

THE RESULTS WERE IN, I am indeed pregnant... two and a half months to be exact. This isn't how I envisioned bringing in my 31st birthday. Especially after Dean told me his original plans of taking me to Hawaii, but after I became sick, he decided a weekend staycation at the Ritz would be a better plan. I agreed, the thought of being on a plane throwing up nonstop didn't seem exciting at all.

My weekend of pampering was off to a great start. First was a full body massage and mud bath, next Dean and I ate lunch at their restaurant that overlooks Central Park. Throughout the day he surprised me with random gifts too. The first gift I received was a pair of diamond earrings that belonged to his mother. At lunch, he gave me a set of Virtuoso paint brushes. After our meal, I wasn't feeling well, so we spent a few hours in our hotel suite. Dean made me a glass of his mother's ginger tea that seems to be the only thing that settles my nausea.

"Today has been amazing. Thank you so much baby." I pulled his arm to lean down and kiss me.

"It's not over yet, baby," he said with a wink. He reached in his bag and pulled out another gift. "From Yaya," he said handing me a small bag.

I smiled as I pulled the paper from the bag. Inside the bad was bottles of finger paint. "It's for you, Yaya, and Nugget to use," he smiled proudly. *Nugget*, that's the name he'd given our bundle of love.

"Aww," I gushed. "We have a while before we can all paint together though."

He shrugged, "Well when that day comes, you'll be prepared."

After two glasses of tea, my nausea went away. Now it is time for dinner and Dean was being very secretive about where we were eating. While getting dressed he stepped into the hall to take a phone call. I wanted to be nosey and eavesdrop, but I don't want to ruin whatever surprise he was working on. When he returned, I got a chance to admire the man who had stolen my heart. Dean wore a pair of olive green khakis and a white polo shirt. He'd gotten a fresh haircut yesterday before we started our staycation. He even granted my wish of keeping his beard, it was getting so long and thick. It perfectly adorned his chiseled jaw. My eyes roamed his body until they landed on his round brown eyes. He licked his lips leading me to believe he was doing the same thing I just did to him. Slowly he sauntered over to me, I licked my lips as he used his index finger to raise my chin. I looked at his full brown lips. He kissed me so softly that I barely felt it. I licked his bottom lip before sucking it.

Dean leaned to my ear and whispered, "After dinner."

When we left the restaurant, Dean reached in his glove compartment and handed me a blindfold. I raised my right brow wondering what he needed that for.

"You trust me?" he asked with a small smile.

"Yes," I said with a light laugh. After I put the blindfold on Dean drove us to our next destination. I was a little annoyed and excited about having to ride with my eyes covered. A few moments I felt the car coming to a stop. I turned to Dean, he rested his hand on my legs before leaving the vehicle. I sat in the car with a racing heart.

Is he about to propose?

We aren't ready for that yet.

My door opened, he unbuckled my seatbelt and helped me out the car.

"Babe, what is going on?" I asked nervously.

"Relax," he said rubbing his hand down my back. I

listened to my surroundings and realized we were still in the city.

Oh, my God.

Please don't propose to me in Times Square.

My stomach turned at the thought of Times Square proposal. Dean walked me through a door, and the sound of the busy city disappeared. I let out a sigh of relief and Dean chuckled as he positioned me in the middle of I don't know where. I heard his footsteps fading out as I stood uncomfortably waiting for the next move. I ran my left hand down my right arm unsure of what is happening. The room smells like fresh paint, which was making me a little nauseous.

"Remove the blindfold," Dean yelled from behind me. Slowly, I took the blindfold off and looked around the room trying to figure out why this place seemed so familiar. Dean turned on the lights and my eyes flooded with tears. The walls were covered with my work. Dean came from the back, and I ran to him. I jumped into his arms, and he spun me around. He held me as I cried the hardest I've ever cried. I had given up owning my art gallery, but he hadn't

"You haven't even looked around, Chubs," he said while laughing. I wiped my eyes before he gave me a tour of my art gallery. It was set-up the exact way I explained to him the first day we came to this place.

"What? How? When?" I asked while shaking my head.

"Don't worry about all that," he ran his finger under my chin. I ran my fingers across every single painting that hung on the walls. Dean pointed to the empty plates beside a painting, "This is where you'll put the name's of each piece." The time and detail he put into making sure my vision came to life had me speechless. I went to the room where open mic nights would be held, the corner stage that he had built is perfect. *Everything is perfect.* I sat on the stool on the stage and envisioned the crowd that would occupy this space every Friday night. My cheeks were hurting from smiling so hard. Dean came in the room and sat in the chair place front and center.

"What do you think?" he asked, his gaze burning into mine.

"It's everything I imagined and more." I walked over to him. "Dean, thank you for being what I never knew I needed."

"I should be saying this to you." The smile on his face reached his eyes, and my heart melted. He kissed me on the forehead, "Let's get back to the room to finish what you started earlier."

I LOOKED around my empty classroom. This last day of school is bittersweet for me. I am happy this chapter is coming to a close on a good note. Now I could devote my time to planning the grand opening for my art gallery. Today was filled with many happy tears and well wishes. My morning class welcomed me with an edible arrangement and a card. My students wrote every weekly affirmation from the school year in the card. It was my goal to motivate and touch them; I succeeded. My last class was the hardest, these babies were upcoming sophomores. I gave every one of them my phone number and made them promise to keep in touch. At the end of the day, I hugged every student as they left for the day. All the teachers, well the ones I had a good relationship with, gave me cards and flowers as parting gifts. Surprisingly, the principal gave everyone in the art and music departments cards as well.

When I finally got home, a bouquet of roses welcomed me on my kitchen island. I already knew the culprit behind it. When I pulled out my phone to call him, I saw Dean already text me.

Dean: The next chapter will be even better! See you and Nugget soon.

I rubbed my stomach while smiling. After a hot shower and a glass of ginger tea, I entered my art studio prepared to finish a painting I started yesterday. Hours later I heard Dean and Yara's footsteps coming down the hall.

"Aunum," I heard Yara yelling. Smiling, I put my palette and brush down to meet her in the hall. I opened the door and here comes Yara running with a teddy bear in hand. Her face lit up at the sight of me.

Scooping her in my arms, I said, "Hi, baby!" She hugged my neck so tight she dropped the teddy bear. I opened my eyes after savoring the hug she gave me, and there was Dean with a big smile on his face. He walked over to us and wrapped his arms around me. With Yara squished in the middle, he kissed my forehead then hers. He whispered something in Yara's ear that made her giggle, then ask to be released from my arms. I watched as she picked up the teddy bear and handed it to me.

"For me?" I said with a gasp. Yara nodded her head before giggling, again. I hugged the bear tightly and said, "Thank you, baby."

Dean chimed in, "She wanted to get you a gift too." I looked between Dean and Yara, thinking about how everything has changed so much since they've both entered my life. We've been through a lot, but I wouldn't trade them for anything. The family we are building is everything I've ever wanted.

EPILOGUE

THREE MONTHS LATER...

ean

TODAY MY BABY is opening her art gallery. I stood off to the side and watched Autumn smile from ear to ear for the cameras. This day was special in more ways than one. She opened her art gallery on her mother's birthday in honor of Ms. Tammy. When we woke up this morning, Autumn cried tears of sadness and joy. Sadness because she missed her mother, which I completely understood and joy because she was finally living her dream. My baby looks so beautiful as she posed in her white pants and red flowy off the shoulder top, sporting a part in the middle of her curly hair. Autumn glowed more than usual, and few people knew why. Of course, the future Godparents, Grant and Ivy knew, but Chubs isn't ready to share with other people that we are expecting. I recently told Aunt Bee and Uncle Greg. Autumn has done well with hiding her growing belly with loose fitting clothes, but I could see the minor changes her body has undergone. We went to the doctor last week, so far she and Nugget are doing great. Ivy is planning her a surprise gender reveal party. She and I already knew the gender, but Autumn said she wanted to wait a little longer before finding out.

After Autumn gave a small speech expressing her gratitude, she cut the red ribbon and welcomed everyone inside the gallery. The past few months my baby worked overtime to have enough paintings to cover the walls of the gallery. She was able to have former students display their work as well. While everyone mingled, I pulled Autumn to the side to congratulate her once again.

"Chubs, I'm so proud of you," I said before kissing her forehead.

"Thank you for believing in my dream. Without you, there would be no art gallery."

I shook my head. "No, it was going to happen with or without my help." After we hugged, she returned to her guests. Autumn took her time showing everyone each piece of art on the wall and a quick story behind it. Her former student, Rayna did a presentation on a series she did just for this opening. Autumn's eyes sparkled as she adoringly watched Rayna speak. Although she hasn't said anything about not teaching anymore, I know she misses it.

The grand opening was coming to a close, but I had one last trick up my sleeve. I looked to Grant and Ivy, and they gave me a nod. After grabbing Autumn from a conversation she was having with Aunt Bee, I led her to the stage. Ivy and Grant were working on getting everyone seated and quiet.

"What are you doing?" Autumn whispered through a smile.

"You'll see," I said with a chuckle. Once the room was filled I took the mic to speak, "First, I want to publicly congratulate my baby on the opening of Art is Love Gallery. She has dreamt of this for years and to finally see it come to fruition is beautiful." Autumn smiled as she joined everyone in applause. "This room will be used for open mic nights and other intimate events. I wanted to be the first to use this room before anyone else," I said making everyone laugh. "I'm no Langston Hughes, but I have a few bars I want to share." I turned to Autumn, and everyone else in the room disappeared,

"THE MOMENT I laid eyes on you I knew you were the one

Yara is my moon, and you are my sun

Your rays brighten my life and my heart

I was foolish in the past, and it almost ripped us apart

You showed me what love is and how to let love in

More than a lover you are my best friend

Love isn't perfect it's hard work, and you are worth it

You accept my babygirl and me

For that, I will always be true

Apart of me always felt something was missing and now I see it was you

I told you before you were the missing piece to what I envisioned as the perfect family that was no lie

But we can't all be a family if we don't all have the same last name....right?"

I pulled Autumn's left hand from her mouth. After getting down on my knee, I removed the box that held her silver four carat cushion cut ring from my pocket. Autumn had tears falling from her eyes that made my eyes get a little misty. I cleared my throat before asking, "Autumn Richardson, will you marry me?" She leaned down and hugged my neck. "Is that a yes?" I said into the mic, causing everyone to erupt into laughter again.

Autumn nodded her head and I slid the ring on her finger before scooping her into a tight hug. After I put her down, Ivy and Aunt Bee ran to the stage to congratulate her. I stood off to the side beaming with happiness as I watched Autumn show everyone the ring.

With the angel from my chain in hand I whispered, "Ma, I know you're proud of me. You knew Autumn was the one."

Grant walked over with my father, both of their expressions showed the happiness they felt. My father held Yaya in his arms, they quickly grew a bond that was one of a kind. Yaya loves her Gramps. I thought it would take her a while to warm up to him, but the first day she met him she hugged him so tight tears formed in both me and my dad's eyes. I felt guilty for keeping them apart for so long, but I've learned as long as you are above ground you have time to mend broken relationships as well as start new ones.

"You really wrote that poem," Grant asked while laughing.

"Yes, and she loved it," I quipped.

My father nodded before saying, "Remember they come first." He said pointing at Autumn and Yara. Our relationship has grown so much over the last few months. I missed his wisdom and guidance more than I wanted to admit. The day I told him my plans to propose to Autumn he shared the story of his proposal to my mother. The first time he asked she said no because they just got back together. He said he was thankful she turned him down because it gave him more time to grow. I kept that in mind while planning this proposal, but the joy on Autumn's face proves this was the right time to take our relationship to the next level.

After the gallery opening, we came home and watched Yaya's favorite movie, *Coco*. Not even an hour into the movie both Yaya and Chubs were knocked out. I looked at Yaya who was asleep on my right side. Then, at Autumn who was sleeping on my left, she had on a sports bra letting her round stomach show. I kissed them both on the forehead before I rubbed Autumn's stomach. She moved and opened her eyes.

"Why are you still awake?" she whispered.

"Can't sleep. Plus, I enjoy watching all my babies sleep peacefully."

She smiled before replying, "We love you."

"I love you all. Everything I'll ever need is right here."

The End.

ACKNOWLEDGMENTS

I want to first thank God for this gift. Next, my *momager* for believing in me and dreaming bigger than I could ever imagine. Lastly, Tamara, thank you for helping make this story come together and for wanting to help in any way!

GIVEAWAY

To enter for a chance to win a signed paperback and an amazon gift card, join my facebook group (The Rosebush) and post a picture of your review in the group. The winner will be announced on **October 1st!**

STAY CONNECTED

Stay up to date on the latest with D.Rose:
Subscribe
Email: **Authordrose@gmail.com**
Join my Facebook Group:
The Rose Bush
Check out the Playlist I made for this novel
HERE